YOUNG
CANNON

SADAAM HASAAN

Dedicated to Aunt Rachel and Sugar. Rest In Peace!

ACKNOWLEDGEMENTS

First and foremost, I have to give thanks and express my gratitude to the Higher Power for giving me the strength, guidance and energy to breathe life into this project. Without God's grace and mercy I wouldn't even be here right now.

My children, Hasaan, Ha'zir, and Lianie... Y'all are my greatest motivation. My two Princes and my Princess. Now-a-days everything that I do I do for y'all. Because of y'all I had to shape up and do the right thing. So, y'all saved me, and I love the three of you unconditionally.

I have to give a special shout out to my Amazing Mother who did her thing as a single mom raising four children. I never really expressed my appreciation in my youth, but as I look back in hindsight, your hard work, strength, and resilience was admirable. I Love You Ma!

Shout out to my brother from another other and business partner K-Bang. You did that time with your head up and your chest out, and you touch real soon. I'm going to have the red carpet rolled out for you my nigga!

Shout out my Bro Dan for being in my corner when no one else was in sight.

Salute to the Big Homie Perc!

Last but not least, I'd like to thank my fans and supporters for riding the wave. None of this would be possible without y'all...

#100k #Thuglife #LOE

-Sadaam Hasaan

"Tee was from the projects, he was only nine/ Every night he would hug his mother when she cried/ Pops wasn't helping out, all he did was lie/ Some nights, Tee was even wishing Pops died....

~ Sadaam Hasaan

CHAPTER 1

"Tee, wake up," Sugar yelled to her nine year old son from the doorway to his room as it was time for him to get up and get ready for school.

"Sugar", whose maiden name was Rachel Marlow, was a thirty one year old, struggling single mother that did whatever it took to provide for her and her only son, "Terrence Marlow", better known as "Tee". Sugar was a mocha complexioned gang-stress, standing 5'3, 154 lbs. with an hourglass figure, light brown eyes, and a pretty face. They lived in Lexington Green Projects, in Newark, Delaware.

"I'm up Ma," Tee replied but hadn't budged and was still laying on his twin sized mattress that had no bed post or box spring. It was just an old mattress on the carpeted floor.

"Come on Boy! You gotta get ready for school!" Sugar persisted.

Tee stretched, yawned, then got up out of the bed and went into the bathroom to do his morning hygiene. After brushing his teeth and washing his face, he went back into his room to get dressed. He only had three good pairs of jeans, four or five good shirts, and one good pair of sneakers, some white on white low-top Air Force Ones that he cleaned with a toothbrush almost everyday after school to keep them fresh. He put on his blue True Religion skinny jeans, a white V-neck t-shirt, his black North Face snorkel, and his Air Force Ones. Once he put his bookbag on his ack, he gave his other a kiss and headed out to his bus stop, which was right in front of his building. There were twelve buildings that made up Lexington Green Projects (Lex for short), and Tee lived on the front line, where all of the traffic came passed.

"Yo Tee, com'ere real quick," one of the high school kids called out from the first floor hallway as he made it to the front of the building from his third floor apartment. It was a kid named "Trev". Trev and four other high school kids were hanging out in the hallway smoking weed and ducking the morning briskness. Tee walked over to the hallway and into a cloud of thick, potent weed smoke that was being blown by the high schoolers. "You wanna hit dis?" Trev asked Tee. Trev was one of the guys that Tee looked up to. He let Tee smoke, drink, and he even let Tee play with his gun a time or two.

Tee reached out and grabbed the blunt. He took a couple pulls, inhaled, allowed the smoke to settle in his still developing lungs for a few seconds, then coughed up the soke, catching an instant buzz from the exotic herbs. The high school kids that Tee considered his oldheads, introduced Tee to smoking weed when he was just eight years old. The school bus that took the high school kids to school always arrived about twenty minutes before Tee's school bus showed up. So, what Tee would do every morning is come outside about 15 minutes earlier than his elementary school peers to catch the high schoolers during their morning smoke session. All of the older guys in the neighborhood took a liking to Tee because of how maturely he conducted himself. Out of all the kids in the projects that were in Tee's age bracket, he stood out the most. Although he was only nine years old, he carried himself like a young adult. He was cool, calm and quiet, but he could be as ferocious as a Pitbull in heat when he was pushed to that point. He didn't care about age or size. Sugar always told hi that "It's not about the size of the dog in the fight but the size of the fight in the dog..." So, Tee wasn't discriminatory when it came to fighting someone who disrespected him. Anybody could get it. Mom Dukes also told him that if he couldn't beat someone with his hands then pick something up and beat them with it. So, Tee was known for knocking dudes over the head with bricks, sticks, and baseball bats when he had to being that fighting came with the territory of living in the projects. People that didn't know how Tee got down were quickly given a proper understanding of where the youngster's heart was at when they tried him.

Tee hung out with the old heads and finished smoking the blunt with them. Trev and the others in the bunch were all about sixteen or seventeen years old and were the young hustlers on the rise. Trev led them. Those high schoolers and a few others in their age bracket from Lex considered themselves the YG's (Young Gangsters). The older and more seasoned hustlers were the OG's (Original Gangsters).

When the high school bus came and went, Tee went to the front of the building and sat down at the bottom of the first floor landing of the stairs to wait on his school bus. His elementary school peers were just making their way out to the bus stop, most of them being chaperoned by their mothers and guardians. Tee was high as a kite! He enjoyed smoking weed, because with his ADHD it mellowed him out. Sugar wouldn't allow him to take the medications that the doctors wanted to prescribe to him for his diagnosis. It also helped him to cope with his living situation. Unlike others his age, Tee was well aware of his mother's struggles, and he empathized with her, feeling all of her pain. Having no one else to lean on, Sugar vented to Tee on the regular basis about her financial endeavors and his piece of shit father, and she cried on his young shoulder almost every night. She had too much pride to vent or cry to anyone else.

No jobs would hire Sugar because of her criminal background, and she couldn't get the same type of government assistance that all the other project chicks got because of her felony drug conviction. When she was eighteen years old, she got caught up in a Federal drug sweep with some major players out of Camden, New Jersey that she was dealing with. Sugar was a key player in the round up, and she stuck to the code by keeping her mouth shut, not telling the Feds anything that they wanted to know or what she knew about her co-defendants. Her stand-up partners rewarded her by taking the weight for majority of the charges. She got stuck with a racketeering and conspiracy charge from being caught on wire-taps. However, her co-defendants testified on her behalf, downsizing and minimizing her role in the operation as much as they were able to, and she ended up receiving a light 36 months in a federal penitentiary. That was nothing compared to the 25 years that the Queen-pin on the rise was originally facing. When she got knocked off, all of her money and assets were seized and placed in federal custody as evidence. She lost everything! So she came home to nothing!

Upon Sugar's release, she started dating a dope boy fro the West-side of Wilmington, Delaware, who supported her all the way up until the time she got pregnant with his baby. That's when he became missing in action. Being the strong woman that she was, she just moved forward without him. Her pursuit to find employment while she was pregnant and with a record was draining and discouraging to say the least. So, when she was five months pregnant, she started selling weed to financially prepare herself for her first child. Sugar had people that she could call for assistance, but she dealt with more pride than the manliest man! Almost ten years later, Sugar was still hustling to provide for her and Tee, but she didn't go anywhere near as hard as she did in her earlier years, because she feared the risk of getting caught up again and leaving her son a parentless child. So, she did enough to get the by.

Tee was no fool. He knew that his other was selling some sort of illegal substance to make ends meet. He didn't know much about the product she was selling. All he knew was that it was some type of hard white stuff that the customers went crazy over! Tee hated to see his other struggling, and he did everything that he could think of to assist. He even sacrificed lunch some days and spent his lunch money on candy and flipped it in school, turning $2 into $5. He would give the money to Sugar, and to her the gestures were humorous and cute. However, he would soon take a leap that she would be forced to take more serious!

"Ma, I'm home!" Tee announced as he returned home from school and stepped through the front door. Getting no response, Tee dropped his bookbag on the living room couch and went looking for his mom so he could tell her about his day in school like he did everyday. He went to her room, and the door was slightly cracked open. He sneakily peeked through the quarter inch crack in the door and witnessed his mother handing three little red baggies of the unidentifiable white stuff to their next door neighbor, an older white lady who everybody called "Mrs. Chrissy." She came over to the apartment almost everyday, sometimes twice a day, and now Tee knew why. He still didn't know what the white stuff was, but he knew that whatever it was, it was illegal and it brought in the money. Tee knocked on the bedroom door, like he wasn't already standing there for thirty seconds, and Mrs. Chrissy quickly stuffed the little baggies in her buxom and straightened up as if the police were coming.

"Come in," Sugar said.

Tee walked in and went to give his mother a hug and kiss, like he did everyday he came home from school. Tee was a true "Momma's-Boy" at heart, and everybody that knew him knew that much. Sugar could do no wrong in his young eyes, and he never left home or came in the house without giving his mother some love. Even if she was sleep, he would peck her on the cheek and keep it moving.

"Hey Baby! How was school?" Sugar asked as she gave Tee a hug and kiss.

"It was good. Hey Mrs. Chrissy," Tee greeted.

"Was sup lil man?" Mrs. Chrissy replied. "Lemme get up outta here," she said as she scurried away.

"Mommy bouta take a nap," Sugar told Tee. "Do ya' homework, then you can go outside and play...." She wasn't too hard on Tee, but she stayed on his heels about doing good in school, because she didn't want him to turn out like the average project kid. Being that she didn't ask for much of him, Tee always listened.

Tee grabbed his bookbag out of the living room and went into his room to knock out his homework. He was done in twenty minutes. He was no slouch when it came to school. He was a straight A student. He didn't love nor like school, but he knew that doing good in school was the one thing that would make his mom happy and put a smile on her face. So, he put his best foot forward in school.

When he finished his homework, he went to let his mom know that he was going outside. He barged into her room and saw that she was asleep on her black futon couch. He kissed her on the cheek, and just as he was about to leave her room, he noticed some clear plastic hanging out of his mom's purse on the coffee table just about a foot away from the futon couch. Tee had never stolen anything from his mother before, and he would never bite the hand that fed him. However, he couldn't resist doing what the voice in his head was telling him to do at that moment. He reached into his mom's purse and pulled out the sandwich bag filled with small red baggies (which he found out later were 12/12 skinnies) of the white stuff. He took five of the little red baggies and threw them in his mouth, tucking them in the side of his cheek, just like he witnessed the old-heads do on the block. Then, he put the sandwich bag back where he found it and left.

Ten minutes later, Tee was standing in front of his building waiting to catch someone that he could sell the white stuff to. He hung out on the block with the old-heads all the tie and was very observant, taking in everything that he heard and saw and storing it into his mental rolodex. So, he knew what type of people bought the stuff and even what to say to negotiate a deal with the customers. The only thing he couldn't figure out was how to get the buyers to come to him, because he wasn't a known hustler, and his building wasn't one of the buildings that dudes hustled out of. The hustlers did sell their drugs on the front-line, because they could stop the traffic before it came all the way into the projects, but it as the front line on the other side of the projects that was jumping.

There were five buildings on the front-line. Two of those buildings were on Tee's side, and the other three were on the other side. The rest of the projects was considered the back, where you had to pull into the projects or walk through one of the front-line buildings to get to. The front-line on the other side of Lex was always poppin'! That's where all of the buyers went. Sometimes they crept through to the back, but Tee's building and the building connected to his weren't known for being places of business. So, Tee started scheming and plotting on a way that he could attract some customers, inconspicuously though, because he didn't want to draw any unwanted attention to himself and let people know what he was up to. If he wasn't doing business with them, then he didn't want them to know his business.

Suddenly, he was struck with an idea. He figured he could walk down to the other side of the front-line, chill with the old-heads, like he did on the regular and wait for the police to ride by as they eventually would. Every time the cops rode down the front-line all of the hustlers automatically scattered and split like roaches when the lights came on, and they wouldn't return for about ten to fifteen minutes when they knew the coast was clear. The little strategist planned on using the window of opportunity to direct some customers down to his building, because when the hustlers dispersed, the customers never stopped coming, and the cops rode by almost every hour just to make their authoritative presence felt.

So, Tee walked down to the other side of the front-line and posted up with the old-heads, both YG's and OG's, after shaking all of their hands. Under the staircase, four or five dudes were shooting craps with money all over the pissy concrete floor. A few cats were posted up on the second floor, looking over the balcony. A couple hustlers stood directly in front of the building, looking to be the first to get to any customer that came through. Customers were coming in and out of the building non-stop. Some of the hustlers were even running up to the customer's cars before they were able to get out. Just like Tee expected, about ten minutes later the headlights of a cop car could be seen coming from about a football field away and got noticed.

"One time! One time!" a few dudes shouted out, alerting everyone that the cops were coming. Everybody hauled ass into the building, and in seconds apartment doors could be heard slamming shut as people were dipping into spots, and just like that the block was vacant. The only person left out there was Tee. The squad car rode right by and left the projects just as fast as it came. Two customers were bending the corner, turning into the projects and walking Tee's way down the sidewalk before the cop even turned off the front-line. It was a middle aged Black man and a Black woman that looked like she was a rough thirty years old. Tee knew what a customer looked like just from paying attention to what went on around him, and majority of them looked bugged out and antsy, like the two that were coming his way.

When they got in front of the building, the female spoke up. "Where ery'body at?" she asked, just speaking out loud, looking around and not paying Tee any mind.

"Come wit' me," Tee told them and started walking down the front-line to his building with the two customers following right behind him.

"Who you takin' us to lil man?" the lady questioned, wondering where Tee was headed.

"Don't worry. I got y'all," Tee simply replied and kept it moving.

They just wanted to get high, and nobody else was out, so they continued to follow him. Tee walked into his building and under the staircase, where he couldn't be seen, and he spit all five bags into his hand. He didn't know what the little baggies sold for. So he decided to just allow their reactions to tell him. He held his hand out with all five saliva covered baggies showing.

"What's these dimes?" the female asked as she grabbed one of the bags with her thumb and pointer finger and squeezed it, paying no attention to the spit that it was covered in. The man was just standing there with his hands in his pockets.

Tee figured that if she assumed that they were dimes then they had to at least be something close to that. So he ran with it. "Yeah."

"Can I get two for fi'teen nephew?" she inquired, looking to work a deal with an inexperienced Tee.

"Nah, I need straight money. This shit drop," Tee pitched, using a line that he heard the other hustlers use on the regular, not having a clue what it actually meant though.

She sucked her teeth, then turned to the man that had been quiet the entire time. "Gimme twenty dollars!" she demanded. He pulled a twenty dollar bill out of his pocket and handed it to her, and she in turn handed it over to Tee. She then took another bag. "You gon' be her for a while?"

Tee threw the remaining three bags back in his mouth. "Yeah, I'll be here for a minute."

"Aright, if it's good I'll be back..." With that said, they scurried away, and Tee posted back up in front of his building. He looked to his right, down the front-line, and noticed that the hustlers on the other side were back out like they never left. He planned on waiting another half hour and repeating what he had just done. However, just when he was prepared to make his way back down the block, the chick and the guy that he had just served were heading his way, back down the front line. Before they made it to his building, Tee dipped under the stairs so he wouldn't be seen interacting with the fiends, and he waited.

"Lemme get three youngin'," the lady said with a twenty and a ten dollar bill folded up in her hand. She was grinding her teeth, and her jaw was moving from side to side, like she was trying to put it back in place.

Tee spit the last three bags out and handed them to the lady. She handed Tee the money and split with the man that she came with right on her heels. In just about an hour Tee made more money than he ever had in his possession at one time in his life. He knew fifty bucks would help his mother out, and he was anxious as ever to put a smile on her face. When he got in the crib, Sugar was still asleep on her futon couch. So he kissed her on the cheek and sat the money in the big aluminum ashtray on her little coffee table.

As Tee was walking out of the room, Sugar felt his presence and woke up. She saw the money sitting in her ashtray and got alarmed. She jumped up, grabbed the money and followed behind Tee. "Boy, where you get this money from?" she barked out of care and concern, wondering what her son had done to get a whole fifty dollars. It was cute and humorous when he hustled up two or three dollars, but this caused her to raise an eyebrow in suspicion.

"I took some of that white stuff out ya' bag. I just wanna help Ma," Tee explained.

"How many bags did you take?" she asked in panic, now hoping that Tee hadn't sold her crack/cocaine for less than what it was worth as those drugs were her only means of providing.

"I took five."

She looked down at the fifty dollars in her hand and smiled as it dawned on her that her nine year old son had just took five dime bags out into the streets and somehow came back in with straight money, something that she was rarely even able to pull off with her needy customers. For a second there, Tee reminded Sugar of his father, who although was a no good man and dead-beat father, could sell salt to a slug and water to a whale.

"Tee," Sugar said in a calm tone. "I understand that we struggling' a lil bit Baby, but you are too young to be out here sellin' crack. This a grown folk's game. I appreciate you tryna help, but let Mommy worry about providin'. Okay?"

"I don't wanna stop Ma!" Tee expressed. "I hate to see you sufferin' all the time. Plus, it's too easy for me. I'm only nine, so nobody even pay any attention to me," he insisted with enthusiasm.

Sugar looked into her Baby-boy's eyes and saw an ambition, deterination, and excitement that she knew all too well. There was nothing she could do to combat what he was experiencing and ultimately what it would lead to. She refused to allow her son to go out into the streets and follow the direction of some half-assed leader, because she knew that Tee falling victim to the streets was inevitable at this point as he had already got a taste, and there was no doubt in her mind that outside influence in the street would have malicious intent and wouldn't have Tee's best interest at heart. Tee was already at-risk just from growing up in the projects, but she could tell that experiencing the rush of fast money had already brainwashed him. So, Sugar decided that she was going to let Tee do his thing but only with her guidance and under her supervision.

"Com'ere Boy!" Sug said and walked back into her room with Tee right behind her. She went into her dresser drawer and pulled out a black 6-shot .22 caliber revolver with a wooden handle. She placed the gun in Tee's open hand. "Don't take this to school, and don't let nobody know you got it. But if somebody try to take suntin' from you, I want you to shoot em...." That was the first lesson that she taught Tee. Then, for the next few hours she schooled him to the crack-game, teaching hi all of the ins and outs and the tricks to the trade without leaving out a single detail!

CHAPTER 2

"What you need Unc?" Tee asked the tall, stocky, bald-headed, African American crack-head named "Dink". He looked like he was fresh home from an extensive prison bid. They were under the stairs of Tee's building, which was no Tee's regular meeting place for his customers.

"Lemme get two," Dink stated in his deep, raspy baritone voice.

Tee spit out two bags and made the twenty dollar exchange. As Dink walked away, he made a parting statement that sounded a bit threatening.

"You better start lookin' out for me lil nigga!"

Tee didn't know if Dink meant that literally or figuratively, but he blew off the statement and posted back up in front of his building. He treated every customer the same and none of the others ever complained. Nobody was treated special, and he wasn't about to start with Dink. Sugar told him to take no shorts and make no exceptions when it came to business.

For two months straight, Tee posted up in front of his building after school and did his thing, making anywhere from two to $400 a day during his six hour a day shifts, Monday through Friday shifts.

He spent his Saturdays and Sundays being a kid. However, as he got deeper in the game, the desires to do childish things began to fade. He was now evolving into a young man.

Sugar still had her New Jersey connections on raw cocaine for a decent price compared to what it was going for, but she only bought an ounce a month that she would cook up into crack. She could've turned up at any moment, but she only dealt with three customers, because she didn't want to put herself out there again and risk being caught. Her customers were super loyal, because she kept them more than happy. While majority of the hustlers in the projects were bagging up $2,500 off an ounce of low quality crack, Sugar bagged up $1,400 of grade A product and sold dimes that were the size of the average twenty dollar rocks. With Tee involved, she still cooked up the coke and bagged it up, and she still dealt with her regular customers, but now she was purchasing three ounces as opposed to just one, because Tee was doing two a month by himself. She had saved up over $3,000, caught up on her bills, and she was even able to treat hard working Tee to a light shopping spree. However, things were about to take a drastic turn!

By following in his mother's footsteps on the business side of things, Tee had gained some loyal customers of his own that came to see him everyday after he got out of school, and they never complained. He was now aware of the fact that he had top of the line product and ten dollar bags that could've easily sold for twenty. Knowing this, he took no shorts, because the fiends were already getting blessed. It was to the point where the customers didn't even attempt to to negotiate deals with the iron-fist youngster anymore. They already knew what it was.

Right when Tee was about to take it in for the night, Dink popped back up. So, Tee went under the stairs to serve his last customer for the night.

"I got a hundo youngin'," Dink said, towering over Tee with a one hundred dollar bill visibly hanging out of his giant hand.

Tee only kept five bags in his mouth at a time. So, he had to go to his stash to get five more. "Wait right here," he told Dink as he walked into the first floor hallway of the building.

His stash was up in the soft-tiled ceiling of the hallway. You could push the tile up, and there was enough room up there to stash almost anything. Before Tee could reach up into his stash, his intuition started speaking, and it dawned on him that Dink never spent that type of money, even if he had it. In the two months Tee had been dealing with Dink, he never spent anything more than twenty dollars. This is when Tee began to question Dink's intentions, and he thought about the threat that Dink made earlier. Tee's instincts were telling him that something wasn't right, and one of the things his mother taught him was to always trust his gut feelings, but before he could react,

"Click-clack!" Tee heard the sound of a pistol being cocked behind him.

Tee turned around, and a big, shiny, chrome, semi-automatic pistol was just inches away from his face, and he was staring down the nickel-sized barrel of Dink's gun. Tee almost shitted his pants in fear, but he fought to maintain his normal, calm composure and not seem too scared.

"Gimme all dat shit lil nigga!" Dink demanded with a scowl on his face, looking like a real live monster. "I want ery'thing!"

"Aight, chill," Tee coaxed with his hands up in submission. "I gotta grab it out the stash."

"What the fuck you waitin' for?" Dink roared. "Hurry the fuck up!"

Tee turned around and went to go reach up into the ceiling stash. As he was feeling around up in the ceiling, he remembered what his mother told him to do if someone tried to take something from him. So, instead of grabbing his pack, he felt around for his gun. He kept the gun cocked. So, when he got a hold of it, he just spun around and pulled the trigger.

"Pow!" the first shot rang out, sounding like a firecracker and catching Dink off guard as it struck him in his chest. With the gun still in his hand and his eyes wide, Dink grabbed for his chest like he was pledging the flag. Tee kept shooting, "Pow! Pow! Pow! Pow! Pow! Click! Click! Click!" He emptied the gun all into Dink's frame and looked into his bulging eyes as he dropped to his knees then fell flat on his face with the gun still clutched in his unresponsive hand. Tee looked down at Dink's body and just knew that he was looking at a dead man. So, before people started coming out of their apartments being nosey and looking to see what happened, he took flight out of the hallway and upstairs to his apartment. He closed the door behind him and pulled the gun out of his pocket. He stood with his back to the door and stared down at the gun in his shaking hand. He was in shock as Dink's dying face began to flash before his eyes.

When Sugar heard the front door slam, she came out of her room and into the living room, where she found her Baby-boy with a blank expression on his face and his gun clutched in his shaking right hand. She could tell from the way that the door slammed that something wasn't right, but now she knew something had went horribly wrong. She calmly asked, "Baby, why you shakin' wit' that gun in ya' hand? What happened?" Her mother's intuition already told her that Tee was forced to bust his gun.

"I just shot Dink Ma," Tee broke out of his state of shock and said. "He tried to rob me."

"Is he dead?" she asked, hoping he was so Tee wouldn't have to worry about looking over his shoulder, or him getting Tee cased up.

"I think so," Tee replied.

"Did anybody see you?" she further interrogated, making sure there was no eyewitnesses that could say they saw Tee kill Dink.

Tee shook his head no. This was what Sugar feared and dreaded, but she knew the day would eventually come when Tee had to prove himself, especially with him being so young. She was just glad that she prepped him well.

"It's okay Baby. Just give Mommy the gun and sit down...."

She took the gun out of Tee's hand and sat down next to him on the living room couch. She hugged and held him for about ten minutes, calmly reassuring him that he wasn't wrong and he did what he had to do. Then, she put the gun in her purse and left the apartment.

CHAPTER 3

"Yo, what you need Unc?" Tee asked a customer as he stood under the stairwell of his building with a walkie-talkie in his right hand. The young hustler was right back at it like he never left with a body under his belt.

"I need two," the fiend said and handed Tee twenty dollars in balled up bills.

Tee got on his walkie-talkie. "Yo, it's one comin' ya' way for two..."

After the Dink incident, Sugar had advised Tee to get his closest friend, "Tweezy" (who was one year older than Tee), to partner up with him to take some of the weight off of his young shoulders and make things run a little tighter and smoother. Tweezy posted up in the next building over from Tee with a walkie-talkie and the product in his possession. The customers came to Tee, where he collected the money, then Tee would let Tweezy know what they wanted and send them over there to get served. Sugar had also instructed the duo to alternate between the two buildings and change positions every few days, so that no one plotting and scheming would be able to pinpoint who had what on them in what building at what time, as she learned from her son being forced to gain his first stripe in the streets.

Tee had knocked off his first 4« ounce order in less than a month's time. Sugar was now copping 4« uonces just for Tee and still just an ounce to satisfy her personal customers, and it seemed as if there wasn't enough supply to meet the demand. Tee and

Tweezy were making an average of six-hundred dollars a day during their six hour shifts. With the traffic that ran through the two front line buildings that they frequented, from 3pm to 9pm, their dealings were no longer a secret to The Hood. So, they were out there on front street now with no shade on their little operation.

It had been a little over two months since Tee bodied Dink, and he woke up in cold sweats almost every night from the nightmares he had about that life changing incident. He saw the face of the man he murdered on the regular. It was like Dink's soul was haunting the young goon, and although Tee kept his tough exterior, on the inside he was hurting!

"Yo, what's good nigga? You aight?" Tweezy asked Tee as they were sitting on the first floor landing of the stairs in Tee's building, sensing that his boy was going through something. Tweezy was rolling up a blunt, and Tee was in a noticeably deep trance.

"Yo, I wanna tell you suntin', but you can't tell nobody dog!" Tee said, badly wanting to reveal what had become his deepest and darkest secret to his best friend. His mother told him to take it to the grave and stressed to him the harmful potential of revealing the secret, being that the law had no statute of limitations on taking someone's life. However, Tee felt like talking to someone would stop Dink from haunting him. Plus, he felt as though Tweezy was trustworthy of confiding in. He knew that Tweezy wouldn't run his mouth or do anything to harm him.

"What is it?" Tweezy asked as he licked around the blunt, putting the finishing touches on it.

"Swear on ya' mom you aint gon' say shit!"

"Bruh, on Mommy I aint gon' say shit!" he swore.

"That was me that killed Dink."

Tweezy just gazed at his friend with his jaw dropped and eyes wide open in astonishment. "Get the fuck outta here!" Tweezy said in disbelief.

"Word up!" Tee nodded and said. "That nigga was tryna rob me."

The whole hood had been trying to piece together who bodied Dink, but couldn't as he was somebody that most of the hood wanted out of the way. So, anyody with a heart could've did it. He was known in the hood for robbing and extorting hustlers and fiends. Nobody would've ever guessed that little 9 year old Tee put Dink in the dirt. First off, he was a little boy. Second, at the point in time of the incident, nobody even knew that Tee was hustling besides Tweezy and the customers he served. It all started to make sense to Tweezy though. Now that he thought about it, his friend had seemed bothered and disturbed over the last couple months, and Dink did get killed in Tee's building right after Tee started hustling.

"Yo, you really bodied Dink?"

"Yeah man, but you gotta keep that shit on the low. Can't nobody know, cause my moms said they can lock you up for a body any time, and I aint tryna go to jail."

Tweezy lit the blunt and took a pull. "I aint gon' tell nobody dog. You know I gotchu..."

CHAPTER 4

"Yo, I'm bouta grab these J's right here," Tee told Tweezy as they were in the Footlocker shoe store at the Christiana Mall doing some shopping. It was Saturday morning, and Tee's tenth birthday had just passed. So, Sugar gave him a thousand dollars to go shopping with. Tee and Tweezy got on the bus first thing in the morning and headed to the mall.

"Yeah, they tough," Tweezy commented. "I think I'mma cop those too." Tweezy had a couple hundred dollars in his pocket from his weekly earnings, and he wanted to spend some money too.

As they were at the front counter getting rung up, Tee's cell phone rang. He looked at the caller id, and it was his Mom. "What's good Ma?" Tee answered.

"I need you to come home right now," she said with a sense of urgency in her tone.

"Aight, I'm comin' now Ma." Tee ended the call. "Yo, we gotta slide."

"Damn! We just got here!" Tweezy said as this was the first store they visited since they had got to the mall.

"I know, but Mom Dukes want me to come home, and it sound like a emergency," Tee further explained. He knew he hadn't done anything wrong. So, he was wondering why his mother was forcing him to abandon his shopping trip and come home. In total suspense, Tee got back on the bus and headed back to the projects with Tweezy following him.

"Yo, what you aint clean ya' room or suntin'," Tweezy clowned as him and Tee stepped off the bus at the top of the road that led to the projects, each with Footlocker bags in their hands.

"You funny as hell nigga. Nah, Mom Dukes prolly just wanna holla at me about suntin'," Tee said as they started walking down the narrow road.

As soon as they stepped foot on the front line, about six or seven unmarked vehicles swarmed them from both ends of traffic, and a gang of detectives jumped out with guns drawn and aimed their way. Both Tee and Tweezy were handcuffed and placed in the back of separate vehicles. They were driven to the New Castle County Police Station. When they got to the station, the officers uncuffed Tee and Tweezy in the booking area and had them sit next to each other on a little wooden bench that was connected to the wall.

Tweezy whispered to Tee, Yo, what the fuck is this shit about?"

"I'on know yo," Tee whispered back. "But whatever it is just keep ya' mouth shut. We'on know shit," he said, letting Tweezy know to keep his mouth shut, no matter what this encounter was about.

"You already know!"

A young, white, clean shaved and neat-suited male detective walked up to the duo and asked, "Which one of you is Terrance Marlow?"

"That's me," Tee spoke up.

"Well, you're wanted for questioning for the homicide of Deandre Washington. So, we have to hold you hear until we talk to you. Your mother's on the way..."

As soon as Tee was apprehended, the detectives contacted Sugar and told her to come to the police station, because it was against the law to interrogate a juvenile without a parent/guardian being present. So, they called Tweezy's mom to come pick him up and waited for Sugar to arrive to start their interview.

Tee was taken to a freezing cold interview room with a bright light and seated at a table by himself. He put his arms inside his shirt to try and stay warm and waited there for about an hour when his mother and the neatly suited detective stepped into the room. His mother sat next to him at the table, and the detective sat across from them.

"Okay, Miss Marlow," the detective started off the interview and pushed a piece of paper and a pen across the table to Sugar. "I'm going to need you to sign this Miranda form, so we can ask Terrance some questions."

Sugar looked down at the Miranda form, then back up at the detective like he had just said something disrespectful. "Ask my son some questions about what?" she snapped, knowing exactly what he wanted to question Tee about, but playing the fool. She had gotten word earlier in the day that the homicide detectives were riding around the hood looking for Tee, which was why she called him and told him to to come home while he was at the mall.

"Well, your son's name has been brought up as a suspect in a homicide investigation, and we need to ask him some questions pertaining to the incident in order for us to clear his name."

"Well," she fired back, showing her hatred for the law in her tone of voice, "I aint signin' no got damn Miranda form! And y'all aint askin' My Baby no mutha-fuckin' questions. We wanna talk to a lawyer," she stated with a twist of her lips and a roll of her neck.

"Okay!" he said in a warning manner. "He has that right, but we're gonna have to place him under arrest until his name gets cleared."

Tee looked at his mother with worried eyes, not wanting to be taken away from home. He looked like a sad puppy, and was wondering why his mother was about to allow this man to take him away from her. His young mind couldn't comprehend the fact that his mother was actually protecting him.

"It's okay Baby," Sugar responded to the terrified look on her son's face.

She didn't want to see her son be taken away to jail, but she was a seasoned vet and knew that asking for a lawyer was the wisest thing to do when being interrogated, especially by homicide. The Miranda rights clearly state, "You have the right to remain silent. Anything that you say or do can and will be used against you in the court of law. You have the right to an attorney. If you cannot afford one, then one will be appointed to you..." So, Tee was just going to have to be strong, because Sugar wasn't about to let him speak so they could use his words against him in court.

"I'll get you back home. Just don't talk to nobody unless I'm there." She gave Tee a firm hug and whispered in his ear, "Be strong Baby!" Then, she walked out of the interview room with the detective following her.

They couldn't legally speak to Tee without his mother being present during the interview and granting consent. However, in the Commonwealth State of Delaware, "hear or say" was all the evidence needed to detain and work towards convicting an individual, especially if that individual didn't have a good team fighting for them. So, Tee was processed, booked and taken to the New Castle County Detention Center, better known as "Bridgehouse"....

CHAPTER 5

Tee walked onto the spacious housing unit full of the hardest and toughest juvenile delinquints from Delaware. He had on some state issued tan khaki pants and a lime green state issued t-shirt with the fresh, black Air Force Ones on his feet that he was wearing when he got apprehended. You could sense the hostility in the air. The tension on the unit was so thick that you could cut it with a knife! Although Tee was a bit nervous, he walked onto the unit with his head up and his chest out. From the looks of things, Tee was the smallest and nine times out of ten the youngest kid on the pod, which only placed a big chip on his shoulder. He was already itching to prove that he had the heart of a wild lion!

He strolled over to the correction officer's desk in the middle of the pod with a netted laundry bag in his hand, containing an extra set of state issued clothes, flip-flops to shower in, a towel and wash rag, a bar of generic soap, and a stick of generic unscented deoderant. Tee felt like every kid on the unit was grilling him, and about 90 percent of them actually were. However, Tee stared them right back down to show them with his eyes that he was just as tough as they were, if not tougher.

"What's ya' name?" the fat, Black CO asked as he was relaxed at his desk, leaning back in his swivel chair with his hands behind his head.

"Terrence Marlow," Tee replied as he stood at the desk and looked around, observing the surroundings as there were many things taking place on the unit. There were five different tables spread out throughout the pod with five or six youngsters sitting at or standing around each table playing some sort of card game. A gang of youngsters were crouched down in a circle on the thin carpeted floor playing what looked like a game of "Hood Monopoly". In the center of the pod, across from the CO's desk, there was a row of young cats who were seated on the green, hard plastic couch watching the big screen TV that was on a metal entertainment center on wheels in front of them.

"Aight, you lock in cell twelve. Go head and drop ya' stuff in ya' cell, and you can come on out for rec..."

Tee walked over to his cell, and the door was already cracked open a bit. He stepped into the small, one man room, and before he could drop his things on the bed, a short, stocky Spanish kid with a curly afro and a missing front tooth popped up at his door, like he was stalking Tee. He was obviously only a teenager, but he looked like he was at least twenty years old.

"Yo, what's good lil nigga?" the Spanish kid asked as he looked Tee up and down.

Tee dropped his stuff on the bed and poked his little chest out "What up?" Tee replied defensively, trying to prepare himself for whatever it was that was about to come his way. He had heard a ton of stories from the older kids in the hood about the things that went down in Bridehouse, and the last thing he wanted to do was become a victim. He refused to be the victim. He'd much rather be the aggressor.

"What's ya' name?" the big guy asked.

"Tee!"

"Aight, they call me Suave. Where you from?"

"Lex!"

"Oh aight! Hold up." Just like that, Suave left the doorway, and Tee was left not knowing what to think.

Did Suave have something against dudes from Lex? Was Suave on his way to round up his goons to give Tee one of the infamous Bridgehouse beatdowns that he had heard so many stories about? Or did dude want his fresh sneakers? Tee didn't have it figured out. However, he had his fist balled up at his sides, ready to go out with a bang if he had to. A few seconds later, Suave appeared back at Tee's cell door, but this time he had company with him.

"You know him?" Suave asked the familiar face standing next to him.

Tee finally let his guard down, eased up and cracked a smile, because the person standing next to Suave was Trev, one of the YG's from the projects. Trev had been locked up for about a month now after being caught with a gun in his possession that was linked to a shooting incident that took place not too far from Lex, where someone was badly wounded. So, he was facing time for the gun and the shooting.

"Oh shit!" Trev exclaimed, cracking a smile as well, just as excited to see Tee as Tee was to see him. "Wassup witchu lil nigga?"

Tee was so happy to see a familiar face in such a hostile environment that he skipped past the handshake and went straight in for a hug.

"Fuck you doin' in here boy?!?" Trev asked as they let each other go and Suave walked off to give them some privacy to catch up.

"They tryna charge me wit' a body," Tee replied.

"Oh yeah?" Trev said in surprise, but knowing that out of all the young boys from the projects, Tee was probably the only one he could see catching a body. "Who they tryna say you bodied?"

"The nigga Dink."

"Damn! That's crazy!" Trev shook his head and said. "I'on even wanna know if you did that shit or not. That aint nobody bid'ness but yours. Whatever happened, take that shit to the grave my nigga. And don't talk to none of these nigas about ya' case. NOBODY! A lot of these fake ass tough niggas be rats on the low, just lookin' for ways to get home," Trev spilled, reiterating some of the things that his mother already told him.

Trev laid down the laws of the land to Tee and showed him how to conduct himself in jail, which was quite simple to Tee. He was basically telling Tee to just be who he was. After showing Tee, who was cool and who wasn't, he told him to mind his business and never back down from a fight, something that he was going to live by regardless.

There were a few more dudes from the projects on the unit, but majority of the jail was from Wilmington, either Northside, Eastside, Westside, Southbridge, or Riverside, and everybody rode with their hood when shit popped off. And shit did pop off!

~   ~   ~

Two Year Later....

"Hey Ma!" Tee greeted and hugged his mother as he came around the rectangular wooden table to give her a hug. They were in the mess hall (cafeteria), which was also where the visits were held on Saturday and Sunday nights. Sugar came to visit Tee every week faithfully to keep him up-dated on what was going on with his case and to show him moral support. Sugar even went as far as seducing a few of the thirsty male CO's so that she could use them to get things in to Tee that the facility considered contraband, like weed, cellphones, and dirty magazines. So, because of Mom Dukes, Tee lived more comfortab;y than his peers.

"Hey Baby!" Sugar exclaimed as she wrapped her arms around and squeezed the upper-body of her rapidly growing son. It seemed as if every time she saw Tee, he grew in both height and weight. He was apprehended standing 5 feet even and weighing 125 lbs. soaking wet. Now, he was 5'6, 175 lbs., and all muscle from the extreme weightlifting, cardiovascular and callisthenic work-outs that he did ritually. He also started growing his hair and wore it in box-braids that were about 4 inches in length, looking like Criss-Cross.

The courts started off trying to give Tee juvenile Life as a plea agreement, which was 7 years in the Commonwealth State of Delaware. However, Sugar wouldn't allow Tee to cop out to the deal. There were no eyewitnesses. There was no murder weapon, and no physical evidence that even placed Tee at the scene of the crime. All the state had was hear or say and circumstantial evidence, and Sugar didn't think what they had would hold up at trial, especially with the lawyer that she invested in to fight for Tee. The prosecutor was now down to his last and final offer, the plea bargain cut off. He put five years on the table. So, it was either take the five years, or set a trial date. If Tee blew trial, the Commonwealth State of Delaware made it clear that they had every intention on waving him up to an adult and giving him the time that an adult would receive for a murder, which would more than likely be 25 years. However, Tee, Sugar and their attorney were ready to fight! They had a strong chance of winning, but the Commonwealth State of Delaware had the same confidence!

CHAPTER 6

"**I**n case number 139-01745, Terrence Marlow versus the State of Delaware..." the young, Asian court clerk announced to the courtroom. After sitting in Bridgehouse for four years and a couple months, Tee was finally at his last and final day of trial, and the verdict was about to be read to the courtroom filled with nosey people from the neighborhood, spectators, news reporters and the jury of 12. "...the state finds the defendant, Terrance Marlow..." There was a pause as the clerk had everyone in the packed courtroom leaning off of their seats in suspense, anticipating what the jury concluded that would ultimately be the determining factor on if Tee would be walking out of the courtroom a free young man or being sent to prison. "...not guilty!"

The entire right side of the courtroom rose to their feet and cheered, like their favorite football team had just made the game winning touchdown, all in support of Tee as he was just deemed a free man by a jury of twelve. Tee shook his lawyer's hand and walked out of the courtroom with his mother by his side and a smile on his face, and he was feeling untouchable!

While Tee was incarcerated, Sugar only had herself to feed and support financially. So, she was able to not only maintain without struggling to do so, but she was also granted the ability to save up about $10,000 as well. She spent a little over $6,000 of that on some coke for Tee to knock off upon his release. As they walked out of the courthouse, Sugar gave Tee a fresh set of clothes to put on and $2,000 in cash to go shopping with. She knew her hustler of a son would get it right back and some in no time at all. She had a dying faith in Tee!

They caught the bus to the projects, and Tee stepped off the bus and onto the pavement feeling like a new kid. He was 5'8, 185 lbs., had shoulder length dreads and a walk that displayed his confidence. He had on some white Robins jeans, an all white Polo button-up and some crispy, white on white shell-toe Adidas.

It was the middle of the summer, and Tee was ready to turn up! When Tee and Sugar approached their building, Tee noticed that his building was being occupied by a bunch of kids that he once went to school with, and they all looked like they were in the mix. One of those kids was no one other than Tweezy. Tee's building and the building connected to it were looking just like the other side of the front line now. Tee didn't like what he was seeing, but like the young G he was, he kept his cool. There were a few oldheads out there too, but it was mostly kids in Tee's age bracket, and even a blind man could see that they were out there trapping. Seeing some of the guys that were out there hustling shocked Tee, because some of them weren't even built for the trials and tribulations that came with the lifestyle, and he knew this for sure being that he grew up with these dudes.

Tweezy, standing ahead of everyone, was the first person to greet Tee. "Yo, what's good my Boy?" Tweezy exclaimed as he opened up his arms to embrace Tee.

"What up?" Tee greeted back and gave Tweezy a hug as his mother ascended the stairs.

Everybody in the building showed Tee love, some with handshakes, some with hugs, and some with both. "I appreciate the love, but I'm fresh out. I know y'all niggas got a couple dolla's for me," Tee said with both of his hands out, looking for everyone that was hustling in his building to pay homage. He felt like it was only right, as he pioneered the flow that they were out there eating off, and this was his building at the end of the day.

They all went into their pockets and placed something in Tee's hand, even if it was only twenty dollars. He ended up collecting about seven hundred dollars from the crowd and went up to his apartment with vengeance on his mind! Although Tee played it cool, he grew to hate Tweezy while he was locked away in that 12x6 foot cell, because Tweezy was the reason why he sat in jail for 50 months for a body that he would've never been apprehended for if Tweezy hadn't ran his mouth. He didn't run his mouth to the police, but he ran his mouth to the hood, which was just as bad, because the hood informants got wind and told. Even though Tee beat the case, that was 50 months of his young life that he would never get back, all because Tweezy didn't failed to honor his word and keep his mouth shut. However, Tweezy was going to compensate for those 50 months with his life! Tee was about to make sure of that. His mind was already set on it.

Sugar cooked Tee a full course meal of the soulfood that he went so long without and missed so much. Sugar could cook her ass off! Her cooking was one of the things Tee missed the most. Her cooking was so bomb that she even sold her home cooked platters on occasions to make a little extra money and had the whole hood chasing her food.

When Tee finished eating, he took the money he collected, along with what his mother blessed him with and headed right back out. He caught the bus back to "The City" (Wilmington). From there, he got on the Septa train to Philly and went to King Of Prussia Mall. He bought two pairs of sneakers, two pairs of Constructs, and about 5 outfits of the latest fashion. He grabbed a few jars of some OG Kush while he was out in Philly too. His next stop was this oldhead chick's apartment in the projects named, "Valery". As Tee was leaving the projects earlier that day, she gave him an invitation to her apartment, seeing that his weight was up and he was shining like a diamond with VVS clarity!

Valery was a twenty six year old project chick with two kids and living off of government assistance, like most of the chicks that lived in the hood. She was a dark chocolate skin complexion and was short with a rocking body and an average face. She was one of those women who used her physical assets to get what she wanted out of the young boys on the rise, like Tee. However, she wouldn't be able to just chew Tee up and spit him out like she did with the rest of the young testonsterone driven. Tee was different! Sugar had told him all about women of Valery's kind when he first started hustling. So, if she tried that shit with Tee, she would end up being the one to get chewed up and spit out.

Tee dropped his bags off at home, then went to the back of the projects to see Valery. "Knock-

knock-knock!" Tee knocked on Valery's second floor apartment door and anxiously waited for her to answer.

"Who is it?" Valery screamed as you could hear her stomping towards the door.

"It's Tee!" he yelled back with a bass in his voice that puberty had just awarded him with just a little over a year ago.

"Who?" she said, as she was now right on the other side of the door.

"Terrence!" he re-announced after realizing that the lady he once called, "Miss Valery" only knew him by his government name.

She swung the door open with a quickness with her honey blond Remi weave hanging down to her waist, a baby white t-shirt on, some Victoria Secret boy-shorts and some black Nike ankle socks. "Hey Boy! Come in," Valery said, then spun around and switched away with an extra twist in her volutuous hips, knowing that Tee was looking.

Tee followed her in and shut the door, his main focus being her trembling ass as it shook and jiggled like jello with each and every step she took. He was in so much of a trance that when she stopped just short of her bedroom door, he accidentally ran into her from behind.

"You okay?" she asked playfully, knowing Tee was just zoned out on her backside.

"Yeah, I'm good," he said, feeling a bit embarrassed but playing it off.

"My kids is wit' they dad right now. So, I got a couple hours," she hinted then stepped into her room.

"Aight, so what you tryna do?" Tee aggressively asked, getting straight to the point as he followed her into the master bedroom.

"Look at you, gettin' all grown and shit," she responded, liking his aggressive approach. She sat on her Queen size bed, facing Tee, as he stood directly in front of her to where she was at eye level with his waist. "You had some pussy before?" she questioned, hoping and praying that he was a virgin. She wanted to be his first so she could turn him out and have him fiending for her, like she was crack and he was the addict. That's how she had all of the young boys, and after the first hit, she made them pay for that crack.

"Yeah," Tee lied through his teeth, wanting Valery to think that he had some type of sexual experience under his belt so she wouldn't think less of him.

"You ever had ya' dick sucked?"

"Yeah," he lied again.

Without saying another word, she undid Tee's belt buckle and unbuttoned his jeans. His young but impressive manhood was already standing at attention just from the mere thought of his first sexual encounter being seconds away. He just looked down and waited to feel the sensations that he had heard so many stories about while he was in Bridgehouse. Dudes quickly grew to respect Tee while he was in there, but when the joke was on him, he caught hell for being the only person who admitted to being a virgin in the detention center. Let all the other juveniles tell it, they were all skilled vets at having sex and smashed more chicks than they could count. Valery ended up sucking Tee off until he nutted in her throat. She gracefully swallowed that, got him back hard again, then gave him the ride of his young life!

Forty-five minutes later, Tee was rolling up a blunt of that OG Kush that he bought while he was in Philly. He then got dressed and lit it up while Valery was still laying ass naked in bed. He blew it down and saved Valery a little bit more than a roach for herself.

"Yo, I'm bouta slide. That was fun though," Tee told Valery, who was damn near burning her lip, trying to smoke Tee's leftovers.

"Where you goin'?" she whined.

"I'm bouta go get to this money. I'll slide back through to kick it wit' you when I find some time though..." Tee vacated Valery's spot and walked home feeling like he just evolved from a boy to a man! The pussy and head that he just got was wonderful and all, but all he could think about was slaughtering Tweezy. In Tee's eyes, his ex-friend was just as guilty as a rat. So, he had to treat him like one.

"Hey Baby!" Sugar greeted Tee as he stepped into the apartment to her sitting on the living room couch watching the big plasma screen TV. "Where you comin' from?"

"I was just out Ma."

"Mmm-hmm," she replied as she cut her eyes at her son and looked him up and down with her lips twisted. Tee went in the kitchen to make himself another plate, and Sugar kept going on. "Don't be out here fallin' for these bitches traps Tee. Remember what I told you. All they gon' want is ya' money," she dropped a jewel, knowing her son was becoming a young adult and now had sexual desires. She knew that there was no stopping a young boy from meeting his needs, especially when they had grown women throwing pussy at them. However, she also knew how these scandalous women were. So, she was just making Tee aware. "And make sure you wearin' condoms, cause I'm too young to be somebody grandmother."

"I know Ma!" Tee said as he was making his plate, not wanting to have a conversation about sex with his mother out of all people. He was taking heed to what she was saying and all, but he had already slipped up by sliding up in Valery raw. However, it was something that he would never do again.

"And you aint ready to be no father," she continued her lecture.

"Okay Ma," Tee said as he stepped into the living room with his plate in hand, looking to end the conversation and move onto something that was more important to him at the moment. He sat down next to her on the sofa. "I'm tryna handle that situation," he changed the subject, talking about what he was ready to do to Tweezy. He had been anticipating handling this for years!

"Wait till tomorrow...."

CHAPTER 7

This was uncommon for Tee, but he slept in late the following day, not waking up until about two in the afternoon. Afrter 4 years of sleeping on three inches of cotton with one eye open, he appreciated his little twin sized mattress with no boxspring or bedpost. Compared to what he just came from, it felt like he was sleeping on air. He woke up to the aroma of his mother's brunch and again remembered that he was home and no longer in the jail cell that he had become conditioned to awakening to. The feeling was great! He took a quick shower, did his morning hygeine and got dressed. He threw on some tan True Religion cargo shorts, a crisp, white, snug-fitting v-neck t-shirt, and his white on white shell-toe Adidas with no socks on.

By the time he made it to the dining room, his plate was already on the table with a glass of orange juice next to it, a simple scene that had become a fantasy of his over the years. When he sat down, Sugar came out of the kitchen and sat at the other end of the table with a plate of her own.

"Mornin' Ma," Tee greeted, then dug into his food.

"Mornin' Baby," she greeted back.

"I'm ready to take care of that today Ma," he told his mother, anxious to tie his only loose end.

"I know Baby! You just gotta make sure you do it right. Don't let nobody see you wit' 'em either. Make sure he dead too, and leave 'em in The City somewhere..." Mom Dukes went on to school Tee on how to go about sleep-walking then killing his former childhood bestfriend and exactly how to get away with doing it.

"I got it Ma," Tee insisted as he had premeditated this murder long before his victory in court.

When they were done eating, Sugar gave Tee an all black plastic Glock 17, which was light, but extremely powerful and had a hair trigger. Tee placed the gun on his hip and headed out. His first stop was the corner store, where he purchased some blunts and some black, leather baseball gloves. He left the store and put the gloves on, thinking to himself, "Let the games begin!"

Tee jumped on the bus headed to The City, then got on the Septa train to Philly. From the 30th Street train station in Philly, he caught a cab to Hunting Park in North Philly, where you could always find the best herb that Philly had to offer. He bought five bags of Purple Kush and got back on the bus, getting off on Roosevelt Boulevard, right in front of a fancy five star hotel.

So far, everything was moving in cadence with the night's plans. It was 6:30pm and just about time for the next step in Tee's plans to begin, which was to get some transportation. His reason for coming all the way to Philly to fulfill this part of the mission was so he could slide through the projects inconspicuously with an unknown vehicle that had Philly tags. He walked up to the gigantic hotel, passed the valet, through the transparent rotating glass doors and into the hotel's spacious lobby. Tee felt out of place as the lobby was full of citizens that were a part of a class that Tee couldn't identify with. It would've been physically impossible for this young hooligan to blend in with this hotel's upperclass patrons. So, he thought hard and fast and dipped into the men's employee bathroom.

He hid in one of the stalls for almost two hours before finally looking through the crack in the stall door and finding who he was looking for, the valet parking attendant taking his bathroom break. There was no one else in that bathroom but the two of them, so the timing was perfect for what he planned on doing. He listened and waited until he heard the man using the urinal. After the man flushed the toilet, Tee pulled his pistol from his waist and stood up. He watched through the crack in the stall door as the man went to the sink to wash his hands, then burst out of the stall with his Glock aimed at the valet's head. "Lock the door, then strip nigga!" Tee barked.

"You got it Big Bruh," the grown man told teenage Tee out of fear as he walked with his hands up over to the bathroom door and locked it like he was directed to do. Then, he followed the second command and stripped down to his boxers. He did it in less than 30 seconds and threw his hands back up.

Tee threw the valet's clothes on over his own. He took the valet's license and threatened to visit his home address if he ran his mouth. He told the valet to wait twenty minutes before exiting the bathroom then left out to go play the role of the valet. Dressed as a valet, Tee waited outside of the hotel for a car to pull up. He took the first car that pulled up, which ended up being a money green Range Rover Sport, tinted all the way around with 28 inch Five star Giovanni rims.

He headed back to Delaware, but got rid of the valet clothes before going back to the projects. He then sent a bum into the liquor store to get him a bottle of E&J. After that, he drove through the projects looking for Tweezy, the tinted windows masking his identity. His old friend was in front of his building with the same guys from the day before. Tee just rode around in the area, waiting to catch Tweezy by himself and out of pocket.

An hour later, while Tee was breezing down the front line for about the third time, he caught Tweezy walking down the sidewalk of the front line by himself, headed in the direction of the corner store. So, Tee beat him to the store and parked without getting out of the car. He watched Tweezy enter the store and come back out a few minutes later with a little black plastic bag in his hand with whatever he purchased inside. Tee rolled down the passenger window just as Tweezy was about to diddy-bop past the truck.

"Yoooo..." Tee yelled, getting Tweezy's attention and causing him to look his way.

Tweezy loooked through the passenger window, and once he saw that it was Tee behind the wheel, he opened the passenger door and hopped in just like Tee predicted he would do. Tee looked around in the side and rearview mirror to make sure no eyes were on him as this was the last time Tweezy would be seen in this area, and he didn't want that last time being seen in the hood to be with him, not with his reputation as a soul snatcher.

"Oh shit!" Tweezy exclaimed, excited to be in a Range Rover. "Dis you?"

"Nah, this a rental," Tee fibbed.

"Yo, let's shoot Up Top," Tweezy suggested, Up-Top being what people in Delaware called Philly. That's where all of the young boys went when they got behind the wheel of a car. Philly to Delaware is like what New York is to New Jersey.

"For what?" Tee asked, not wanting to go back to Philly after what he had just done out there. "I gotta a bottle of Erk and Jerk and some Purple Kush I just grabbed from Hunting Park earlier."

"Oh aight! Where that bottle at though? cause I'm tryna get fucked up!" Tweezy said as Tee pulled out of the store's parking lot.

Tweezy was always trying to get fucked up, even when they were younger. That's what he spent all of his money on. Tee used to tell him that his desire to always want to be drunk and high would be his downfall, and that premonition was about to be proven correct. Tee grabbed the bottle that was in a little brown paper bag in between his legs and handed it to Tweezy to bust open.

"We bouta go to The City to bag some hoes," Tee stated with hoes actually being the last thing on his mind. All he could think about was morder! Revenge was Tee's prize, and he had his eyes focused on it! He couldn't move forward until Tweezy was gone at his hands.

As Tee drove to The City, the bottle was being passed back and forth. However, Tee was perpetrating the fraud. He didn't drink. He didn't like the way alcohol made him feel. So, he acted like he was sipping from the bottle, but was really just allowing Tweezy to do all of the drinking. By the time they got to The City, Tweezy was twisted, in the passenger seat running his mouth with slurred speech and an empty E&J bottle in his hand.

"Yo, I love you my nigga!" Tweezy claimed as the alcohol brought out his emotions. "I couldn't wait for you to come home," he went on.

"I loved you more my nigga," Tee replied, knowing that Tweezy was too incoherent to be aware of him using the word love in the past tense. Tee actually did love Tweezy like a brother, but there's a thin line between love and hate, especially in this case. Tee couldn't wait to put Tweezy down for good. Watching a bullet pierce his skull would've given Tee a hard-on at his point in time.

Tweezy continued to babble and run his mouth belligerently, slurring to the point where you could no longer understand what he was saying. So, Tee drove to a school playground on the Eastside. It was dark and quiet outside. Tee got out of the car, and

Tweezy followed behind him, stumbling behind Tee into the playground, still running his big mouth.

After making sure they were the only people in the park, Tee whipped out his pistol and turned to face Tweezy, who had laid down on the park bench and continued to chatter away. He was too out of it to even see himself being lined up. Tee cocked his pistol, "Click-clack!"

Tweezy turned his head Tee's way at the sound of the pistol being cocked and stared right down the barrel of the Glock that was in Tee's gloved hand, catching one right to his forehead, sending a chunk of his brain matter and blood flying every which way. Tee followed up with a succession of shots that ripped through his face and head. "Blocka! Blocka! Blocka! Blocka! Blocka!" Tee dropped the gun on top of Tweezy's lifeless and damn near decapitated body and jetted back to the truck. He drove back to Newark, ditched the SUV down the street from Lex and took it in for the night.

YOUNG CANNON

CHAPTER 8

"You gotta put six grams of bakin' soda on every twenty eight grams to bring back a good amount and still have some drop," Sugar educated Tee as she measured out the baking soda on the handheld digital scale that was sitting on the kitchen counter. She then dropped the baking soda into the 16 ounce Pirex measuring cup that had the 28 grams of coke in it. "Now, I'mma cook this one, but you gon' cook the next one And make sure you pay attention, cause if you fuck this up, that's ya' money you fuckin' up."

Tee watched his brilliant teacher of a mother attentively as she stirred, whipped and created crack-rocks out of powder cocaine, baking soda, heat and a flick of the wrist. Tee took into account every detail of his mother's veteran cooking skills. When she was done, Tee was a bit nervous about messing up his first batch, but for the most part he was ready. Twenty minutes later, he had succesfully whipped up his first ounce with precision. A chef had just been born!

After Tee took care of Tweezy, Sugar presented to Tee his first nine ounces of coke. She taught him how to cook the coke into crack, because manufacturing your own product is what gives a dealer their power. You have no creative control buying crack already cooked up, and you're basically just taking your supplier's word that the product is good. However, when cooking your own coke, you can make it grade A, or you could stretch it and maximize on your profit margin. Sugar cooked up nothing but the best, which is why the few customers that she did have would always be loyal to her.

"Now, this that drop," Sugar said, implicating that the crack was top notch. "Watch this!" She grabbed one of the solid golf ball sized rocks off the papertowel covered porcelain plate with her latex gloved hand. She held it up over her head and dropped it onto the hard tiled kitchen floor. One would've thought that this man-made rock would break or crumble, but it smacked the floor with a thud and looked like it hadn't even been tampered with. Tee picked up the rock with his gloved hand and closely examined it. He said to himself, "This all it takes to make people go crazy!"

Later on that day, Tee was back out there, but this time looking to lock down the projects, and he had already conjured up about ten different marketing strategies to do so. He was starting with plan A, which was building up a supreme clientele and getting the dudes that hustled in his building to either roll with him or roll out.

Sugar and Tee had cooked up that whole nine ounces. Tee bagged up individual grams in sandwich bags and decided that he was going to put them on the market for $45 a piece for whoever came to get them, both fiends and hustlers. The fiends were automatically going to flock to him with those prices on such good product, and the project hustlers ran into so many droughts that as long as Tee was consistent (which he would be), they too would eventually come crawling to him at some point.

"I see y'all out here," Tee acknowledged as he came down the stairs to the group of middle school and highschool kids that were hustling in front of his building, eating off the flow that he pioneered. "Where my boy Tweezy at?" Tee asked, knowing firsthand where he was, but strategically playing the inquiring mind.

"I'on know," one of the loitering teens replied. "I aint seen the nigga all day."

"Well, I got grams for forty-five, and I'm out here," Tee calmly stated and walked off with a Nike knapsack on his back that contained the nine ounces of bagged up crack, a hand-held digital scale and a nickel-plated, semi-automatic Smith & Wesson .45 caliber with an extended clip that was filled with hollow tips. He walked back to Valery's spot. Her kids were running around the house, so he knew getting some pussy was out of the question. That wasn't his intent anyway. Instead, he had a proposition to present to her.

"So, wassup Young One?" Valery said as she sat next to Tee on her black leather living room sofa. Tee took the knapsack off his back and sat it on his lap.

"Roll this bud up," Tee demanded, handing her a twenty dollar bag of Purple Kush and a Backwood.

Tee flipped through the channels on her TV as she rolled up the blunt. Her son's, one being three years old and the other one being four, mischeviously ran around the apartment half-naked with little nappy afro's.

"Where you get this weed from?" Valery asked as she lit up the blunt of Kush and inhaled the first pull, not accustomed to smoking the finest.

"That's Purple Kusg. I got that shit from Up-Top."

"This some kill," she said, meaning it was good. She passed Tee the blunt then coughed.

"Ayo, I gotta easy way for you to make a couple dolla's real quick," Tee began to pitch, then took a few pulls and held in the smoke until it started to put a strain on his lungs.

"I aint sellin' no drugs for ya' lil ass. So, you can forget about that," she said, jumping to conclusions.

"Nah," he replied, releasing the cloud of smoke that he was holding in. "I just need you to hold some shit down for me, and I'mma give you two-fitty a week." He passed her the blunt back and continued. "I know you can use a lil extra change. That's a stack a month that somebody else gon' get if you don't jump on it."

"When I'm gon' get paid?" she asked, already biting the bait.

"I got ya' first two-fitty right now. All you gotta do is tell me you on deck." Tee pulled a knot of money from his pocket and started counting out bills with the blunt hanging from his lip, waiting for her to say she was on deck.

She stared at the money with hunger and desperation in her eyes, then put her hand out for her first payment. He paid her before pulling the 250 grams of cook-up out of his knapsack. It was in a big Ziploc freezer bag. He took out 10 of the individually bagged grams and gave the remainder of the quarter key along with the scale to Valery to put up.

She stashed the work in her bedroom closet and gave Tee the spare key to her apartment just in case he ever had to get to his stash when she wasn't home. Tee had just solidified his first traphouse....

CHAPTER 9

"**G**imme forty grams," Tee told Valery as he sat on her couch, puffing on a blunt. He was about to head back out to cover the orders that his customers were waiting on.

Tee had been home for a little over 90 days, and he was "That Dude" in the projects! He allowed dudes to hustle in his building and the building connected to it, but only if they followed his rules and regulations. He felt that he had the authority to set his own rules and regulations being as though dudes were shitting where Tee was eating. His rules and regulations were to buy off him, hustle for him, or pay a weekly homage. He spoke to everyone individually, and no one contested his ruling, because even though the state wasn't able to prove at trial that Tee murdered Dink, everyone knew he did. And just knowing that Tee was willing and able to kill made most fear him and others respect him. They definitely didn't want to try him. So, everyone just fell in line.

Valery stepped back into the living room with a sandwich bag in her hand that had the 40 separately bagged grams in it that Tee requested. "You need anything else?" she asked as she handed Tee the bag.

"Nah, I'm good," Tee replied, then passed her the blunt he was smoking. "You aight though?"

"Yeah, I'm aight."

With that said, Tee put the coke in his knapsack and threw the knapsack on his back. Along with the coke for whatever orders he had lined up, Tee also kept in his knapsack his gun and a ski-mask. He also kept a baseball glove on his right hand (his shooting hand) in preparation for the many unfortunate possibilities that come with the lifestyle he was living. If his hand was ever forced to bust his gun on some spontaneous shit, he would have the tools to do it right and not too recklessly.

Tee was now buying a half a key every two weeks and was paying twenty seven dollars a gram from his mother's connect, a price that he knew for sure nobody in the projects was paying anything close to. He made eighteen dollars profit off each gram. He had ten fiends that came to see him everyday, spending nothing less than the forty-five dollars that he charged per gram. Then, he had the dudes that were trapping for him in his building and the conjoined building. Last but not least, he had the other project hustlers, even the OG's, coming to him for twenty and thirty grams here and there. Tee was up $50,000 and still climbing, because there was still so much more money to be made! His crack had the hood in a frenzy! It was looking like the 80's all over again out there. Competition was nonexistent, and there was only a handful of hustlers in the projects that didn't purchase their product from Tee, probably out of pride and ego. The crack practically sold itself.

Tee had another chick in the projects, whose apartment he made his second traphouse. Her name was "Ariel". She was in her late 20's and stood 5'2, with a petite body frame, light skinned and a pretty face. With Tee's G'd up conduct and irresistable sway, there wasn't a chick in the projects that he couldn't hit. So, he ended up dicking Ariel down, and had her stashing shit for him as well for $250 a week. She lived in the building connected to Valery's building. Every time Tee re'd up, he stashed a quarter key at each traphouse, so he wouldn't have all of his eggs in one basket if shit ever hit the fan.

As Tee was crossing the parking lot, which split the back of the projects in half, to make his drops,

he ran into Trev, who he hadn't seen since
Bridgehouse. He was fresh home from a 4« year bid
for that shooting that he had ended up getting
cuffed for.

"Oh shit!" Tee exclaimed, happy to see his
oldhead. "What's good nigga?"

"Yo, what up Young Cannon?" Trev greeted
and did the project handshake. "I heard you that
nigga out here. Lemme hold suntin' for the hoes get
it."

"Shit! The hoes aint gettin' this," Tee joked
back. Without question or hesitation, he went right
in his pocket and handed Trev a bunch of
unorganized bills. "That should be like five hunnit
right there."

"Good lookin' lil bruh. I see you out her off ya'
shit too. I'm diggin' that," Trev complimented as he
stuffed the money in his pocket.

"I'm just tryna make it bruh," Tee claimed. "I gotta couple drops to make real quick, but I'm out here if you need me for anything..." Tee gave Trev some more dap and kept it moving, on his way to conduct some business with a few of his regulars. One was an oldhead that hustled on Tee's side of the projects, but in the back. He bought ten grams every few days. Another was a young boy that was Tee's age, who trapped in the front of his building. Tee fronted him ten grams a week. The last two people he was going to see were two of his loyal fiends, and they put orders in for five grams a piece. That wasn't an average order for a smoker, but these weren't your average smokers. They were the ones that wisely spent a decent amount of money each time so they could make their money back then smoke the rest of what they bought. These two fiends repeated this process as often as they could, which was usually everyday, sometimes two or three times a day. Tee was The King of his little twelve building jungle no doubt, but being the one who

reigned supreme didn't mean that points no longer
had to be proven!

CHAPTER 10

"**B**oc! Boc! Boc! Boc..." Tee awoke from the unmistakable sounds of rapid gunfire. It wasn't unusual to hear shots ring out in the projects, but on this particular night it sounded like someone was shooting right outside of his window. So, Tee instinctively grabbed his pistol from under his mattress and went to go look out his third floor window with just his boxers on to see what was happening.

He peeked through the blinds with his gun down at his side as more shots went off, and he stole a glimpse of the two masked gunmen, wearing all black that were shooting at the front of his building where dudes posted up at while they were back-pedaling to their getaway car. The car was parked right in front of the building. It was a champagne colored Chevrolet Malibu. The shooters jumped in the car and burnt rubber down the front line and out of the projects.

It would've been foolish for Tee to go investigate the incident right then and there, as the police would be responding to the shooting within minutes. So, he laid back down with every intention on looking into the situation as soon as as the sun rose.

With the shooting fresh on his mind, Tee wasn't able to get a good night's sleep. So, it was a restless night for him, but at the crack of dawn he was dressed and ready to head out for the day. He left his strap in the crib, which was something that he rarely ever did, as he'd usually rather be caught with it than without it. However, he knew that law enforcement would definitely be lurking after the previous night's shooting. Tee usually minded his business, but being that the shooters victimized Tee's building, it was only right that he made it his business.

When he got to the front of his building, it was vacant and so was the conjoined building, but fiends were still out and about, lingering and looking oblivious to what went on just hours ago and probably not even caring as they were just focused on finding their morning fix. Tee was mindful that the block was probably being surveilled. So, he walked through his building and into the back, looking to see if someone could shed some light on the incident that Tee was in complete darkness about. He spotted one of his workers that trapped in front of his building walking across the parking lot, coming from the other side of Lex, and the little 13 year old boy looked like he was petrified.

"What's good G?" Tee asked Lil Gary, who was about 5'3, less than 120 lbs. and went by the nickname, "G".

"Yo, niggas robbed me last night," G explained. "And them niggas slammed on me!"

"Oh yeah?" Tee said in surprise as if he didn't know anything. "You aint slam back?" Tee had equipped G with a brand new Colt .45 revolver when he first put him on, and instructed him to keep it on him at all times. So, Tee was wondering why last night's events transpired without him hearing the loud boom from the .45 caliber.

"Them niggas caught me slippin', so they got the strap too."

"You let them niggas take ya' strap?" Tee went on in a disappointed tone of voice, causing G to put his head down in shame. "Come take this walk wit' me..." Tee led G to Ariel's apartment building. Tee used his key, and they walked right into her first floor apartment. He went straight to the kitchen, and G followed. Tee pulled a chair over to the kitchen counter and stepped on the chair so he could look over the top of the cabinets. He reached up to the space on top of the cabinets and pulled down an all chrome automatic .32 caliber Tech with a swiss cheese nozzle and handed it to G. He then pulled down another automatic, an all black Mac-90 with a 50 round drum clip attached and stepped down from the chair.

"What them niggas get you for?" Tee asked.

"Like four-hunnit and a few grams."

"Who else was out there wit'chu?" Tee further interrogated, looking for answers.

"Ummmm..." G thought "...Trip, Jay and Black, but Black got away though."

Tee was trying to get down to the bottom of what happened, and the first sign of suspicion had already arose. The dude "Black" was prime suspect number one with three strikes against him. Even if he wasn't the culprit behind the robbery plot or involved in it somehow, he was about to catch a bad case of mistaken identity. His first strike was him being the only person that got away, and he wasn't robbed. Second, he wasn't from Lex. Third, he was from Southbridge, which was a hood in The City that had an M.O. for doing out of town stick-ups and setting people up. The bottom line was that somebody had to pay for the loss. Not because it hurt Tee's pockets, because it didn't, but because someone had to pay out of principle. He had to send out a violent message. If he didn't respond aggressively, then it would more than likely happen again. So, Tee was ready to make an example out of anyone that he felt as though would make the best example, and it was looking like that would end up being Black.

~ ~ ~

"You ready" Tee asked G as they were parked in the retirement home parking lot right across the street from the projects. They were in an old, royal blue, stolen Crown Victoria that was tinted loose. Tee was in the driver's seat. G was in the passenger seat, and they were facing Tee's building. They were both dressed in all black attire with ski-masks on their heads and machine guns in hand.

It was a little after 10pm, and the block was still jumping as usual. Junkies were copping and moving, and the young hustlers were out there competing with each other, seeing who could convince the most customers to put money in their pocket instead of their competitor's. It had been a few weeks since G got robbed and shot at, and he hadn't been back on the block since that night, as he was told by Tee not to show his face in the hood so it would look like he was bowing out. Contrary to what others may have thought, Tee and G spent those few weeks investigating the previous incident and plotting on how they would go about getting at Black. Through their researching, they found out through word of mouth that Black was the one who set up the robbery, proving Tee's suspicions to be correct. Being that Black was the mole and the only one of the culprits that they had the drop on, he was going to be the one to get dealt with to send a clear and direct message to the stick up boys that, "Lex niggas weren't to be fucked with!" They had been parked in the old folks home parking lot since two in the afternoon watching the building.

"Yeah, I'm ready when you are," G replied, however, not really being as ready as he said he was. G was no bitch, but he had never busted a gun before. This was going to be his first time putting some work in. So, he was quite nervous. He wanted to put the work in and handle the problem so that it wouldn't re-occur and he could get back to the money, but he had those nervous jitters that you get before facing any challenge for the first time in your life.

"Click-Clack!" G cocked the Tech back, sliding a bullet into the chamber. Tee did the same and pulled out of the old folks home and into the projects. He had the Mac-90 in his right hand and was steering with his left. He parked on the side of his building, right next to the big green project dumpster and cut the headlights off. They stepped out of the car in unison with their ski-masks pulled down. They ran through the grass towards the front of the building with their guns steadied, like they were some sort of special ops, and they were both ready to shoot. Fiends and other bystanders that were out and about hauled ass down the sidewalk or into the building after seeing two masked men with machine guns on the prowl. Tee led the way all the way to the front of the building, where he caught all five occupants of the building slipping with their guards down, but his only focus was the intended target, who was on the third step with a bottle of Hennessey in his hand and a burning blunt in his mouth. As soon as Tee locked eyes with Black, the infiltrator turned around and started running up the stairs, trying to make it up to the second floor landing, but Tee chopped his down, hitting him all in his legs and dropping him at the top of the stairs. The rest of the crowd wisely dispersed. Tee walked up the steps until he was about six steps away from Black's sprawled out but still squirming body. Tee looked back at G, who was right on his heels with his gun aimed at Black, but he was frozen.

"Knock that nigga shit off!" Tee demanded.

G quickly stepped ahead of Tee and stood over Black with his machine gun steadied. Black spun around on his back and put both hands up, like he was going to block a bullet, begging for mercy. However, there was no mercy, no sympathy, and once everything was said and done there would be no remorse! G held down on the trigger and started firing, the machine gun shaking in his little hands and vibrating his body as he shot through Black's hands and into his forehead and nasal passage, opening up his entire face, like he was receiving plastic surgery. Tee bailed back to the car with G following. They headed to a hotel that they had rented for the night, where they also had a legit car waiting.

They left the guns in a car a block away from the motel on "The Ave." (New Castle Avenue), in New Castle and set it ablaze.

CHAPTER 11

"**A**yo, we bouta slide through Crofton real quick," Tee told G as he pulled out of Lex in his new money green Lexus GS coupe with a popular artist from Delaware named "Sadaam Hasaan" booming from the sound system. "I gotta go see what's good wit' this nigga Dealz. That nigga aint pay his dues this week, and he aint even come holla at a nigga or nothin'."

It had been over six months since Tee and G put that work in on that dude Black, and Tee ended up making G his right hand man. He didn't give him this position because he felt like he was the best right hand man to have. He only did it because they committed a crime together that the law has no statute of limitations on. Tee wanted to keep G close by, because he feared and worried that G would run his mouth like Tweezy had done and get him cased up again. Tee knew the possibility of him beating another body was slim to none. He didn't even want to go through those motions again. So, he kept G around at all times just to be safe.

Tee had recently bumped his order up to a whole key, in which he was knocking off in no more than two weeks time. He had also started dumping work off on dudes in some neighboring townhouses called Villages of Crofton (Crofton or V.O.C for short). A whole quarter of his order was getting moved out there. The rest got knocked off in Lex. G's job was simple. All he had to do was stay by Tee's side and do what he was told. Tee rewarded him by keeping money in his pocket, providing him with the finest herbs to blow, bringing him in on the hoes, and shopping sprees once a month when

Tee went shopping. Everything that Tee was rewarding G with was only being done because he didn't trust the little nigga, and he wanted to keep him close by with his guard down at all times. Tee figured that he could use G for whatever else he was worth while he was around as well.

"Oh, aight. Bet! It's whatever," G replied, letting Tee know that he was down for whatever was about to transpire, badly wanting to prove his loyalty as he still felt as though it needed to be proven with all that Tee did for him.

Tee pulled into one of Crofton's many entrances and drove down to the end of the street that he pulled onto. From just riding through the quiet, suburban neighborhood one would never come to assume that illegal activities took place out there, but it was actually where majority of Lex's supreme clientele resided. There were customers for every drug under the sun in Crofton, and there were some youngsters (some from Lex) that posted up behind the scenes in Crofton, trapping and stopping the money from getting to Lex. When Tee found this out, he didn't try to force the young entrepreneurs to stop intervening with the money that came to Lex. Instead, Tee decided to just corner the market by feeding them the work on consignment, and it proved to be a lucrative venture.

Dealz was a 17 year old hustler, who was originally from Westside, but lived in Crofton and had a few traphouses out there that he hid out in and frequented to move his product He didn't know this, but Tee knew about all of the spots that Dealz operated in and out of, as that was required information in Tee's eyes. So, with the company of G, Tee made his presence felt at all of Dealz' spot, seeking his whereabouts. However, he came up with nothing. Once Tee realized that Dealz was ducking him, Tee just laughed to himself as he pulled out of the neighborhood.

~ 113 ~

See, Dealz could run and hide, but he couldn't hide for long, especially not in the little state of Delaware. He would eventually end up turning up somewhere. One thing was for certain though. When Tee finally did catch up with Dealz, there was no more talking. Dealz was in for a rude awakening! The nigga only owed a few thousand dollars, which could've easily been worked off if Dealz would've just been real and explained whatever his delimma was to Tee. Workers fucked money up every other day. That was a part of the game that Tee understood. However, Dealz killed his chances to make things right by ducking. He had dug his own grave. Now he had no choice but to man up and lay in it!

CHAPTER 12

"Yoooo..." Wacko yelled through his end of the phone as Tee answered on the receiving end.

"What up Bruh?" Tee asked as he cruised down Rt. 273, on his way to meet up with some thots over Northside with G riding shotgun.

"Ayo, I got the drop on that nigga you was lookin' for," Wacko claimed.

"Where you at?" Tee inquired, ready to abort the initial mission that he was on so he could go collect this intel on Dealz that he had been waiting months to come across. Tee was well known, and loved by most of the people that knew him. So, he knew once he put the word out that he was on the hunt for Dealz, it would only be a matter of time before someone revealed the coward's whereabouts.

"I'm on The Ave.," Wacko replied.

New Castle Avenue, better known as The Ave., was a main avenue that ran through a major part of New Castle and was also known as Cash Ave. It made its name for being a goldmine for every illegal hustle you could possibly think of, from prostitution to heroin distribution.

Wacko was a comrade of Tee's. He was a thorough young dude from Crofton that Tee grew up with. Wacko was just a year older than Tee. They went to elementary school together, but they really got fly from the years they did in Bridgehouse together. They lived like brothers in Bridgehouse. If you fought one, you had to fight the other. Wacko got booked when Tee was two years into his apprehension, and he was charged with a body as well that he ended up beating from a lack of evidence. Wacko had cooked a customer that owed him money. He went home a few months before Tee did, and he was getting to the bag! His thing was the heroin though.

"Aight, I'mma hit you when I get close to you," Tee said before ending the call. "Ayo, Wacko said he got the drop on that hoe ass nigga Dealz. So, I'm bouta pull up on 'em real quick," he informed G.

"Oh yeah?" G said in surprise.

"Yeah, we bouta see what he talkin' bout. We'll catch up wit' them hoes some other time..." Tee started heading in the direction of The Ave. Fifteen minutes later, he was breezing down the prostitute and fiend infested strip. He texted Wacko and told him that he was on The Ave. Wacko texted right back and said to meet him at the McDonalds across the street from the Motel 8.

As Tee continued cruising down The Ave., he was already thinking about what he was going to do to Dealz and how he was going to do it. Tee stayed equipped with a .45 caliber Berretta on his hip and kept a 2.23mm AK-74 in his trunk at all times. Not to mention, the 7mm Sig Sauer that he had G holding down with a trained instinct to shoot first and ask questions later. Tee pulled into the McDonalds and him and G went inside. He texted Wacko letting him know he was there as they ordered something to eat and took seats.

Less than a minute later, Wacko walked in, looking just like a young winning dope-boy. He was fresh to death with red and black Balenciaga everything on from his shirt to his shoes. He had a Chicago Bulls snapback on, a gold ropechain and a bust down Brietling on his wrist that was flooded with diamonds. He was a light brown skin complexion, 5'9, 175 lbs. with a medium build, a clean, low haircut with waves, and he was tatted loose. At just 16 years of age, Wacko was worth every bit of a hundred thousand.

Tee and G stood up to greet Wacko with their neighborhood handshake that consisted of two smacks of the hand and an embrace. Then, they all sat down.

"So, what's the word?" Tee inquired.

"Man, that nigga Dealz been all up and down The Ave the passed few days Bruh," Wacko stated. "I been catchin' that nigga bustin' traps at the carwash. I started to just line that nigga myself, but I kinda figured you wanted to knock that nigga shit off ya'self"

"You got the drop on the nigga?" Tee asked.

"I'on know exactly where that nigga at right now, but I know we can catch that nigga slippin' at the carwash. That's facts!" Wacko assured.

"You tryna mob?" Tee asked Wacko, seeing if he wanted to get in on some action. Tee and Wacko had never put this type of work in together. However, they both knew where each other's hearts were at. Wacko was a known threat from terrorizing the streets on his rise to fame. In their neck of the woods, Tee and Wacko were the most feared and respected kids in their age bracket. It wasn't that he needed Wacko to mob with him, but he wanted him on this mission to solidify some shit.

"Nigga, you know I'm tryna mob!" Wacko confirmed. "A nigga violate you, he violate me. Straight lace! You know what's goin' on."

"Aight, bet!" Tee said, rubbing his hands together in anticipation. "We gotta get a jonny though...."

~   ~   ~

"You sure that nigga gon' slide through here?" Tee asked Wacko, who was in the passenger seat of the "jonny" (stolen car) that Tee bought from one of the young car thieves from the hood. Tee was behind the wheel, and G was in the back seat of the all black E-350 AMG Mercedes Benz truck. They were all equipped with heavy machinery and wearing all black everything with leather gloves on, skully hats and black bandanas tied on the lower halves of their faces. It was 9:30pm, and they were parked in the back of The Ave.'s most popular carwash, where Dealz was said to have been seen serving his customers regularly over the last few weeks.

"Yeah Bruh!" Wacko affirmed. "I'm tellin' you, I been catchin' that nigga meetin' up wit' fiends almost everyday over this muh-fucka."

"Aight, so we just gon' squat here then till the nigga pop up," Tee stated.

They sat there in silence for about a half hour before they spotted someone that fit Dealz' description with a hoody and a skully hat on. He was walking their way with two junkies in tow.

"Ayo, I think that's him right there," Wacko pointed out as the trio came into sight about 20 yards shy of where Tee had the truck parked behind the carwash.

"Yeah, that's him," Tee confirmed. "Come on, let's go!" Tee stepped out of the car with a black MP5 Heckler & Koch submachine gun clutched at his right side. Wacko and G stepped out at the same time as Tee, both with F&N Mag machine guns clutched at their sides, leaving the car doors open so they could jump right in and make a fast getaway when it was time to roll.

When they were all out of the car, Dealz stopped in mid stride and squinted their way, trying to figure out who these suspect looking dudes were that were quickly pacing his way. He saw guns and thought it was a stick-up. So, he spun around and started power-walking in the opposite direction while reaching for the pistol on his hip. The junkies just stood their, completely unaware of what was going on, and wondering why Dealz just did an about face.

Tee saw Dealz reach for his waist as he was walking away. So, before he got too far away or whipped out a pistol, Tee raised his gun, aimed and started spraying. The fiends scattered.

"Tat-tat-tat-tat-tat..." Wacko and G fired off as well. "Tat-tat-tat-tat-tat..." Dealz tried to run, but before he made it ten feet, he was chopped down from the force of the multiple bullets that struck him from behind. Tee, Wacko and G all ran forward to finish him off, neither of the three being the type to leave a mission incomplete. Although Dealz was laying still and inert on his face, they stood over his body and let him have it, riddling his frame with bullets.

They then ran back to the truck, and out of nowhere Wacko turned his gun on an oblivious G, delivering two shots to the back of his head, doing what he had discussed with Tee earlier in the day. Tee killed two birds with one stone and gave birth to his new official right hand man!

CHAPTER 13

"**A**yo, what you tryna do this weekend?" Tee asked Wacko as they sat in Valery's living room doing the usual, each smoking a blunt of loud to the face and counting money.

Tee was selling crack, and Wacko was selling heroin, but they still rolled together, and they were as thick as thieves. Where one was, the other was never too far behind, and the on-lookers both feared and hated the dangerous collaberation. It had been about four months since the death of Dealz and G, and although the hood suspected that Tee and Wacko were behind the murders, there was no proof. Denzel Washington said it the best in the movie "Training Day" when he said, "It's not what you know. It's what you can prove..."

Tee's sixteenth birthday was just a month ago. He was now purchasing two keys a week, and he sold nothing less than an 8-ball (3.5 grams) a transaction, in which he sold for $135 a piece. He was the weight man for the entire Newark and New Castle, Delaware, and being that he was the man at such a young age, he acquired a whole lot of haters. Even the dudes that he once considered his oldheads, their handshakes were no longer matching their smiles. However, Sugar told Tee that this would happen long before he became the man. Tee had earned his right to be the man though. So, he felt like the streets had no choice but to respect it.

"I was gon' shoot out Jersey to holla at my cousin about these straps," Wacko stated.

"Where he at out there?"

"He in Plainfield."

"That's the cousin you was tellin' me about, right?"

"Yeah Bruh!" Wacko said, nodding his head to add emphasis. "This nigga the slammer man. He got them hoes too. So, if you tryna pull up wit' me, we can grab some jawns and fuck some bitches."

"You tryna slide out there now?"

"I'on give a fuck. Bring a few bands witchu though if you tryna grab some straps..."

Tee and Wacko drove out to Plainfield, New Jersey with Wacko riding shotgun in Tee's Lexus. Tee brought $2,500 with him in hopes of buying some heavy machinery. He already had an assortment of guns in the cut that he picked up here and there along his travels, but there was always room for more artillery. War could be waged at the drop of a dime in the streets, and Sugar embedded in Tee's mind early on that proper preparation prevents poor performance! So, although war wasn't wanted, it had to be anticipated, or else, if and when it came he wouldn't be prepared for it.

Their first stop was Wacko's cousin's house on 4th and Plainfield Avenue, on the Westend of Plainfield. Jersey had better weed than Delaware. So, before stepping into Wacko's cousin's house, Wacko took Tee down the street to the corner to buy some of the block's known exotic herbs. Wacko bought a few 20's, then they walked right into his cousin's two-story house.

"Oh shit!" A bald headed, light skinned duded with a sunni beard, teardrops on the right side of his face and a red bandana tied on his head exclaimed, as he was sitting on the living room floor with a Playstation 4 joystick in his hand and a strap with an extended clip hanging out of it in his lap. "What up witchu lil nigga?" He stood up and tucked his strap on his waistline.

"Shit," Wacko replied. "I told you I was gon' pull up on you soon. This my bruh Tee right here. And Tee this my cousin Shotty." Shotty exchanged nods with Tee and gave him some dap. Then, he gave Wacko a hug.

"I know you gotta be a official nigga," Shotty said to Tee, "cause Wacko don't never bring niggas to my spot. So, what y'all tryna do?" he asked.

"You know we tryna get some straps cuzzo. What you got for me?" Wacko said.

"Nigga, you know I got whatever you want as long as ya' paper right."

"My bread always right," Wacko said, pulling a thick stack of money out of each of his front pockets and holding them out in both of his hands. "Bruh tryna get some shit too though. We came band up."

"Aight, come take this ride wit' me...."

Wacko and Tee followed Shotty out of the house and into a burgundy Dodge Durango that was parked in the driveway. Wacko got in the passenger seat, and Tee got in the back. Shotty turned the music up and drove a few blocks over, parking in front of a boarded up house. Wacko and Tee then followed Shotty around to the backyard of the abandoned looking house, where Shotty stuck a key into the lock of a cellar door. They walked down into the cellar of the house, and Shotty closed the cellar door behind them.

"This aint the same spot you took me to before, right?" Wacko asked as they walked down into the pitch black basement. You couldn't see a thing.

"Nah," Shotty said as he flipped the light switch, illuminating the basement and revealing eight fold-out tables with blue tarp covering them. "I operate outta the bando's. So, I switch spots every few weeks." He went around snatching the tarp off of each of the tables. It looked like a gun show down there. Almost every make and model was on display, causing both Tee and Wacko's eyes to light up like kids in a candy store. "That shit keep me under the radar," Shotty elaborated on the question Wacko asked. "Lemme know what y'all niggas want, and I'll give y'all a play..."

Handguns were no longer a commodity in the streets, unless you had a ladder (extended clip) hanging out of it. I mean, niggas carried them, but you had to have a Mac or better in these days and times, because even the little niggas had big guns, and they were shooting! So, Tee and Wacko bypassed the pistols and went straight to the tables full of machine guns. Wacko grabbed an all black AR-15 with a drum clip attached to it and a folding stock. He unfolded the stock and examined it while Tee picked up a Thompson assault rifle (Tommy Gun) that also had a drum clip hanging from it. Wacko ended up purchasing the AR-15 and two Draco's. Tee bought two Thompson's and a plastic

Glock 27 with a 30 round ladder. Shotty broke down their choices of artillery and put them in two separate gym bags.

After shopping for artillery, Shotty went and picked some chicks up and showed Tee and his cousin to a good time. Tee and Wacko ended up staying the whole weekend, bullshitting and partying with Shotty, just enjoying the fruits of their labor, something they rarely got a chance to do as they had the streets of Newark and New Castle as their responsibility.

CHAPTER 14

"Boom!" there was a loud thump on Valery's door, sounding like a battering ram was colliding into the door as Tee and Wacko were sitting at the dining room table smoking and joking. After that first Boom, they both jumped up and off instinct reached for the pistols on their hips, even though they knew it was the law. "Boom!" With the second bang, you could see the door coming off its hinges. They both ran towards the back room, and Tee opened the window, ready to take the second floor leap with Wacko right on his ass, waiting to follow his lead. However, when Tee looked down, there were suited up SWAT officers with assault rifles aimed up at the window, leaving them with no choice but to surrender. Now you could hear the door coming down and the law announcing their presence.

"New Castle County Police! Search warrant!" they srceamed upon entry.

Tee and Wacko both knew the drill. So, before the cops even made it into the back room, they quickly pulled their pistols from their hips, tossed them in the closet, and laid down on the floor face first with their hands on top of their heads. They were cuffed, searched and escorted out to the parking lot, where they were thrown in two separate squad cars while Valery's apartment was ransacked and ripped apart by a bunch of officers who were in search of drugs and guns that they had been getting intelligence from their informants and anonymous tips on. The cops found four handguns, each with extended clips, two assault rifles, hollow tip ammunition, a quarter key of cocaine, 600 bundles of heroin, a quarter pound of weed, and $27,000 in cash. Tee and Wacko were taken to the New Castle County Police Department, where they were kept separate and thrown in cells. They both exercised their right to remain silent and waited to be arraigned and granted a bail.

Eight hours later, Tee and Wacko were both brought in front of a judge for an arraignment. Sugar was already there, and she brought her Black lawyer with her to represent her son and his partner in crime. This was the same lawyer that beat Tee's murder case. They were both charged with everything that was found in the apartment. They pled not guilty, and they were both given $250,000 bails, cash or bond. The attorney had a quick word with his clients before they were escorted out of the courtroom by two officers.

Sugar yelled to Tee and Wacko as they were being taken away, "I'm comin' to get y'all ASAP!"

Sugar was Tee's bank, and was in possession of Tee's entire $225,000 savings. That wasn't even including the money that was still owed to him on the streets. One of Sugar's old friends was a bails bondsman. So, instead of 10 percent, she would only have to pay one percent with a co-signer. It was 5:30pm. She went straight home to gather up the money and find a co-signer, and she had their bails paid before 8pm. She then went to pick them up from the detention center.

~ ~ ~

"Good lookin' Ma," Tee thanked his mother as he sat in the passenger seat of her Cadillac CTS that she purchased as a result of Tee's hard work.

"Word up! Good lookin' Miss Sug," Wacko followed up from the back seat.

"Y'all know I got y'all," Sugar replied as she pulled away from Bridgehouse. "Y'all know somebody told on y'all, right?" Sugar said, stating the obvious, but making sure they were aware of the fact that somebody was conspiring with the police to get them out of the way. Somebody had to be telling. It couldn't have been the way that they were moving, because they didn't hustle directly out of neither one of their traphouses in Lex. They were strictly stashspots and sometimes a place to kick their feet up. "What y'all need to do is find out who tellin' and handle that shit before they tell on y'all again," she further advised.

They both figured somebody was telling, but still they listened to Sugar's wise counsel as she went on to explain how they could go about figuring out who ratted them out. Getting rid of the snitch wouldn't get rid of the charges that they had hanging over their heads and pending. That was a whole nother fight. However, they weren't about to stop hustling because one of their spots got raided, but they couldn't just go full throttle again with the person that got their spot raided on the loose.

Whoever it was could easily get the drop on them again and get them brought up on more charges. So, they had a process of elimination to do in order to get down to the person that told on them.

CHAPTER 15

Tee and Wacko still had work stashed at Ariel's apartment, in the next building over from Valery's building. No charges were pressed on Valery, but she was evicted from the projects for her involvement and her not telling on Tee and Wacko. She kept her mouth shut, even after they threatened to take her kids away. Tee and Wacko hit her with $10,000 a piece to find a new living arrangement and have a couple dollars to get ahead. They had other traphouses in the area, but Lex was their headquarters. The duo decided to get their work out of Lex and stashed it in Crofton until they got rid of the person that dropped a dime on them. If they got caught up in another raid like the previous one they would be finished.

"Man, fuck dat!" Wacko expressed. "We should just cook anybody that look at us funny." They were chilling in Ariel's smoking some loud.

Tee started dying laughing at Wacko's outrageous idea. "If we did it that way, we would have to cook the whole hood, cause none of these niggas handshakes be matchin' they smiles..." Tee witnessed the hate and envy everyday, but if he was to act on every sign of hate and envy that he witnessed, he would be sentenced to death, because the whole hood was hating on him and Wacko. He was no fool. Sugar had put him on all of the signs of envy and hate. So, he could spot a hater coming from a mile away. He was a Young Cannon that had the hood on smash, kept a big gun on his hip, and people who tried to cross him always got mysteriously crossed out. Who wouldn't want to get him and his right hand man, who was just as devious and dangerous, out the way?

"I'm bouta go get some more Backwoods," Wacko said as he got up, grabbed Tee's keys and left the apartment.

Tee laid back on the couch and ended up nodding off. When he came back to, he checked the time on his phone. An hour had passed since he dozed off, and Wacko still hadn't returned from his trip to the corner store, which was only a two minute trip. He didn't have any missed calls or text messages from him or anything. So, Tee was a bit concerned. He took his Glock 27 with the 30 round clip out of his knapsack, cocked it back and placed it on his hip. He threw a glove on his right hand and put his ski-mask in his back pocket. He then left Ariel's in search for Wacko. Before Tee stepped all the way out of the building, he noticed that the parking lot was flooded with cop cars. So, he quickly doubled back, put the strap up, and went back out to investigate, having a gut feeling that whatever it was that was going on Wacko was somehow involved. The whole hood was outside, standing around in front of the buildings being nosey as usual.

"Who got bagged?" Tee asked one of the female onlookers.

"They got ya' boy. They said he had a gun on 'em," the chick claimed.

"Damn!" Tee uttered, thinking to himself that the last thing Wacko needed was another strap charge, but at least he would be given a bail. It was just a gun. Tee went up to his crib to talk to his mother about getting Wacko out of the jam that he was in. He really wanted to go post his boy's bail before he even made it to Bridgehouse.

"Ay Ma, they bagged Wack wit' another strap," Tee told his mother as he stepped into her room.

She was lounging on her futon couch, zoned out, watching TV. "I know Baby. I heard," she replied, like it wasn't a big deal.

"We gon' bail 'em out, right Ma?" Tee inquired, thrown off by his mother's nonchalance.

Sugar took her attention away from Tee and looked him in the eyes. "He not gon' have a bail that we can pay this time Tee. They got 'em for a body..."

Tee didn't know where his mother got this information from, but she was never one to just talk about things that she couldn't factually prove. Sugar's word was gold. So, Tee's heart dropped along with his jaw, hoping that his name wasn't tied into whatever body that they were charging Wacko with. He knew Wacko was G'd up, but Tee was still praying that Wacko remained solid and didn't speak about anything that they had done, thinking that he was helping himself out. Tee knew that he himself was a person of interest to the New Castle County Police Department, especially the Homicide Division. They just knew they had to come at him correct, and they couldn't, because Tee put his work in like a veteran. Tee's mind went into over-drive, thinking about Wacko and hoping that he stood up.

"I'mma send the lawyer down there to make sure he don't talk though. I'm bouta call him in a minute," Sugar said to ease the worry that she knew her son was experiencing, knowing how her Baby-boy thought.

"Damn Ma! This nigga left all this dope in one of our traps."

"Get rid of it, and give the money to his mother," Sugar suggested.

Tee never sold heroin before, but he knew majority of Wacko's clientele from always being with him. So, it wouldn't be a problem knocking off the work that Wacko left behind. Sugar called her lawyer and made him aware of Wacko's situation, and he went straight down to the Homicide Division to make sure Wacko's rights weren't violated, especially his fifth amendment right (the right to remain silent). Tee went out to go do some networking to secure some sales for the dope that Wacko abandoned. He was sick that his shadow was gone!

CHAPTER 16

"Yo, what up nigga? You good in there?" Tee asked Wako, who was on the phone, calling from Bridgehouse.

He had been booked for two weeks. He got charged with a body that was almost two years old that Tee knew nothing about. They were claiming Wacko allegedly murdered a pimp that got in his way while he was hustling on The Ave. The victim was popped three times in the face. So, the media was making Wacko look like a heartless monster! The pending charges and the gun he got caught with didn't make him look any less criminal either.

It only made matters worse. His bail was set at 2.5 million dollars, cash only.

"I'm always good nigga. Head up, chest out. You know what's goin' on, What's good wit'chu though?" Wacko said, in good spirits about his current situation.

"Shit, I'm out here for us. I gave ya' Moms that bread too from what you left on the land, and I went and got ery'thing niggas owed. She got all that."

"Aight, good lookin' Bro. Ayo, you thought I was gon' bend on you too! Didn't you?" Wacko questioned, knowing how he would've been thinking if the shoe was on the other foot and Tee got booked for a body.

"I can't even lie Bro, I was a lil worried. We cut from the same cloth though, so at the end of the day, I knew you was gon' stand up."

"Real niggas do real things! Loyalty is everything man! And it's death before dishonor my nigga. Come on. You know the drill!"

"So, what you think shit lookin' like for you?"

"I'on even know right now Bro. I'm waitin' on my discovery to come through, so I can see what kinda evidence they say they got on a nigga. I know I'm definitely gettin' waived up. They tryna get a nigga outta Bridgehouse right now. They said my juvenile record too fucked up. Then I got these pendin' charges. So, shit real right now for the kid, but I'm holdin' it up though."

"Just keep ya' head up my nigga. I'mma do whatever I can for you on the land. All you gotta do is gimme the word, and I'm on it," Tee stated, letting Wacko know he was there for him if he needed anything handled on the streets to better his situation.

"I be knowin' Bro. Ayo, call this lil bitch on three-way for me real quick though..."

Tee made the Three-way call for Wacko and put the phone down so he could have some privacy with the female that he was talking to. Now that Tee had done everything he could for Wacko at the moment and let him know he was on deck for him, he had to get back to figuring out who told on them. He had to get the rat out of the way before getting back to the money. He didn't close shop completely. However, he couldn't operate the way he wanted to with that rat still on the land. So, he wasn't reaching his full potential, and with the charges that he had pending from the raid, he had to stack up as much money as he could to hold Mom Dukes down just in case he had to turn in and do a little bid.

~ ~ ~

It had been three weeks since Wacko got cased up. It was 10pm, and Tee was squatting in the bushes outside of an apartment building, in Windhover Apartments, right outside of Lex. He had on all black everything, a ski-mask covering his face, and his 30 shot Glock 27 in his gloved right hand, cocked and ready to blow. Tee was squatting on Valery's baby-father, "Roc", who lived in the building that he was hiding outside of. He had been crouching there for over an hour waiting to get the drop on this nigga. Roc was in his early 30's and hustled in Lex, but Valery didn't fuck with him at all. The most she did was let him see his sons every once in a while. Tee sold Roc work on the regular, but dude was a sucker on the low. He knew that Roc was jealous of him having Valery on his team. So, Roc was prime suspect number one, and Tee was about to serve him. Tee had been clocking Roc's every move the last few days, and he realized that Roc left the projects at around 10pm everyday and walked over to his Windhover apartment. The walk from the projects to Roc's building was only a few minutes. So, Tee calculated that he would be arriving any minute now.

From where Tee was squatting in the bushes, he had a birds eye view of the front of the building, but he couldn't be seen from the outside looking in. He was blind to the naked eyes.

"I'm bouta bust ya' ass," Tee heard a male voice say to a female that he was walking with.

"Boy, shut up!" the female replied.

When the duo came into Tee's visual, he saw that it was Roc and a young Black chick from the projects. He waited until they walked into the one way in one way out building and crept out of the bushes with his gun drawn and aimed at Roc's back as he was ascending the stairs with his hand wrapped around the young lady's waist.

"Boc-Boc-Boc!" Tee fired, hitting Roc in his back and shoulder causing him to twirl and drop on his back as the chick ducked down for cover and hauled ass up the stairs.

Tee walked up to Roc, who was laid out on his back twitching and put two hollow tips in Roc's head, leaving the dirty gun with the body as he followed all of the precautions to make sure ballistics wouldn't be able to link the gun back to him.

CHAPTER 17

"Tee, what up lil nigga?" Trev greeted Tee as he approached the back building that Trev was posted up in at around 9:30pm. This was the building that Trev commonly posted up in and sold his drugs.

"What up?" Tee replied dryly, looking at Trev sideways with his knapsack on his back and and his hands in his pockets as he entered the building.

Tee was no longer feeling Trev's style, and he had every right not to be digging him. After he hit Trev off when Trev first came home, Trev turned into one of Tee's many haters in the hood. Trev was someone that Tee would've least expected this from.

He thought that if anything, Trev was going to jump on the winning team upon his release, but instead, he allowed his pride and ego to get in the way of him accepting a plate from someone younger than him. So, he starved, and he hated Tee because he wasn't eating, but his starvation was nobody's fault but his own, because Tee didn't let anyone starve that wanted to eat. Now, Trev's pride and ego was going to seal his fate in the worst way.

"Why you lookin' like you wanna flex on a nigga?" Trev said as Tee was mean-mugging him as he stepped into the building headed for the first floor.

"Nigga, aint nobody worried bout you," Tee responded, when in all realness, he was daydreaming about exactly how he was going to gun Trev down.

Trev literally never left the hood. So, Tee had to catch him in Lex, because he was the next one up on Tee's list of suspects that had to be annihilated.

Tee had a gun and a ski mask in his knapsack as usual.

"Don't forget who raised you lil nigga," Trev spat as he sat on the stairs with his phone in his hand.

"Yeah, aight!" Tee remarked as he walked into the first floor hallway of the building. As he was walking through the building, he took off his knapsack, pulled out his nickel-plated semi-automatic 9mm Taurus with the 33 shot extended clip. He cocked it back and threw his ski-mask on. He walked through the other side of the hallway, coming out to tha back of the building. He then crept up the back stairs with his gun in his baseball gloved hand. When he got to the second floor landing, he quietly opened up the hallway door and walked stealthly through the other end of the hallway. He peeked through the hallway window, and saw Trev still seated at the bottom of the stairs. Tee slowly pushed open the hallway door, trying his hardest not to make any noise that would alarm Trev, but the door made a squeaking sound when it opened, causing Trev to look up, killing Tee's element of surprise. Tee aimed and shot, but he was too late, because Trev had already jumped up and took off.

"Fuck!" Tee expressed as he ran down the stairs, trying to catch up with Trev so he could finish what he started. When he got down the stairs and to the front of the building, he heard a shot go off and instinctively ducked, then saw the flame just a short distance ahead of him. It was Trev shooting back as he ran across the parking lot, but aimlessly. He wasn't even looking in the direction he was busting. Seeing that Trev wasn't even accurately aiming his pistol, Tee ran after him, looking to chase him down and finish him off. He fired a few shots at Trev while he was running after him across the parking lot, trying to at least knock him down, but Trev ended up making it all the way across the parking lot and into a building. With twelve apartments in each building, Tee had no idea where Trev could have gone.

So, he was forced to abort his mission for the night and make his way home.

~ ~ ~

Being that Tee shot at Trev but wasn't successful in killing him, he decided to put his mother in a hotel on Rt. 13, and he relocated to a hotel himself, a little further down the highway from her. Tee knew that Trev couldn't fuck with him when it came to the gun game, and he highly doubted that Trev would bring gunplay to his door. However, Tee was taught by Sugar to never underestimate his enemy and always be prepared for the worst case scenario. So, the most strategic thing to do was get out of the hood for the time being. He knew that Trev would be running around telling everybody that he ran him out of the hood, and once Tee went a few weeks without showing his face, people would begin to believe that Tee had met his match and was actually ran out. That's when Tee would pop back up and catch Trev slipping.

CHAPTER 18

"Yo, I need you to bring me a-hunnit," Tee told Ariel over the phone.

He had been staying at The Budget Motor Lodge on Rt. 13 the past two weeks, and he was still doing his thing. He just had Ariel bringing him a certain amount of work a day so he could serve his customers. Tee's plan was working too. The streets were talking and saying exactly what he exprected and wanted them to say. He planned on re-plotting his attack on Trev real soon.

"Aight, I'll be there in a lil bit," Ariel replied.

"Don't wear no panties either," Tee added, feeling fresh.

"Boy, you stupid! I'mma see you in a minute..."

Tee was down to his last thirty grams, and he had a whole day's worth of orders to fill. This was his fifth motel room since he had been out and about. He had been in rooms all up and down Rt. 13 and Rt. 40, so he wouldn't make himself hot by maneuvering out of the same spot. After every day's profit was brought in, Tee was dropping the money off to his mother at her hotel. He had been dicking Ariel down every time she came through with what he needed and hitting her off with cash for holding shit down.

While he waited for Ariel to come through, he twisted up a blunt of some OG Kush to blow with Ariel when she arrived. He then laid back in the bed and thought about how he was going to get at Trev. It took everything in him to not just hunt Trev down the day after he missed his target. However, the Young Cannon was taught by his mother to be a thinker before a doer, unless his hand was forced to do without thinking. If Tee hadn't put an extreme amount of critical thinking into the things that he had done over the years, he would've been locked up for a body or two, or maybe even three.

"Knock-knock-knock!" someone knocked on the hotel room door.

Tee jumped up and grabbed his black semi-automatic Smith & Wesson .45 with the ladder in it from under the mattress of the Queen size bed. He held it down at his side as he went to the door and looked through the peep-hole. It was Ariel with a plastic Wal-Mart bag in her hand. He opened up the door with his pistol still out, but behind his back as he let her in then looked around outside to make sure she was alone and not being followed before shutting the door, and putting the gun back under the mattress.

"Why you so paranoid? Nigga, aint nobody gon' do nothin' to you," Ariel said as she sat the bag on the bed and sat down, kicking off her Jordans.

"Bitch, I aint paranoid. I'm just aware. To be aware is to be alive, and I'm tryna live," Tee shot back, getting that quote from his Moms.

"Whateva Boy! the stuff in the bag, I put a box of sandwich bags in there for you too."

"Good lookin'. Now, get naked." Tee demanded as he took his v-neck t-shirt off with his platinum Jesus piece still swinging from his Cuban.

"Ya' lil nasty ass," Ariel said while she was shimmying out of her leggings and kicking off her socks, getting buck naked just like Tee liked her to be. She got on her knees and elbows and assumed her favorite position, face down, ass up, waiting to be drilled from behind by her young buck.

Tee got hard instantly from the sight of Ariel's nakedness and glistening pussy. So, he unbuckled his belt, dropped his jeans to his knees and crawled behind her. He slid right into her juice-box and started drilling her from behind, trying to murder her pussy like he always did!

"Knock-knock-knock!" There was a knock at the door that caused Tee to pull out in mid-stroke and quickly pull his pants up. He buckled his belt and grabbed his pistol from under the mattress, looking back and forth from the door to Ariel as he made his way to the door. Ariel was under the covers with the blanket pulled up to her face, like she was scared.

Tee switched rooms every few days and had only been in this room for a day, and he hadn't told anyone other than Ariel and his mother that he was staying there. So, he was wondering who this could be at the door. He walked lightly over to the door and went to look through the peephole, but whoever was on the other side of the door had the peephole covered. Tee wasn't about to take any chances with the person who was on the opposite side of the door. He thought worst case scenario, stepped back, raised his pistol at the door and started firing off.

"Boc-Boc-Boc-Boc-Boc!" He then swung the door open and in fell "Lil Tommy", Trev's little brother, flat on his face with a gun clutched in his hand. Tee shot him in the back of the head to make sure he was dead. Trev had sent his brother to try and handle his dirty work. Next, he turned his gun on Ariel. She was balled up in a fetal position under the covers. Tee didn't know if Ariel set him up, or if Trev just caught on to his movements and had his little brother follow her over here. However, he couldn't risk giving her the benefit of the doubt. Plus, she was a witness. So, he emptied the rest of his clip in her.

Tee grabbed the bag of work and made his way out of the room. It was broad daylight, and people were looking his way, peeking out of their rooms, because of the loud shots that had just been fired. He also heard sirens blaring in the distance, but they sounded like they were getting closer by the second. With a quickness, he popped the trunk of his car, dropped the bag of work in. He grabbed his Draco with the 100 round drum clip, cocked it back and jumped in his car. As Tee pulled out of the hotel and onto Rt. 40, a gang of squad cars were on his heels as soon as he pulled out. Tee put the pedal to the metal and swerved through traffic in an attempt to get away from the pack of squad cars that were behind him and right on his ass, but to no avail, as cop cars were coming out of the woodworks to join in on the pursuit.

"I aint goin' back to jail," Tee said to himself as he pulled the emergency brake and fishtailed around to where his whole driver side was facing the oncoming traffic, which consisted of a bunch of cop cars.

He leaped out of the car with the Draco aimed and started swinging it back and forth, dumping at the cops that were coming his way. Traffic suddenly stopped as a few of the squad cars crashed into each other, and a few of them jumped out of their cars, taking cover behind their car doors. Tee let off a few more rounds, then jumped back in his car and put the pedal to the floor.

Tee had slowed down the pursuit by busting at those cops, but they got right back on his heels, and this time they were shooting. Tee decided to take this chase towards Lex, in an area that he knew like the back of his hand so he could hopefully navigate his way out of this situation. He made it all the way back to the front line of the hood, right in front of his building, but there was nowhere for him to go from there. Law enforcement had everything blocked off, like they knew he was coming this way. They also had the helicopter on him now. The Young Cannon had already made up his mind that he wasn't going back to jail. So, as he sat in his car with his Draco in hand, contemplating his next move, he made a split decision to go out in a blaze of glory, taking as many cops as he could on his way out. He reclined his seat and leaned back in it. He then pulled a fresh, fully-loaded drum clip from under his seat and changed clips.

A helicopter was floating over the scene, and the cops were yelling on their bullhorns for Tee to step out of the car with his hands up. He planned on stepping out of the car, but not with his hands up! There had to be at least a hundred cops surrounding Lex with all types of guns drawn and aimed Tee's way. Tee kicked the driver side door open and leaped out of the car, but falling on his back in the middle of the street with his gun already swinging and shooting every which way that he could before they riddled his 16« year old frame with bullets. He went out right in front of the project building that he was born and raised in, like

a   YOUNG   CANNON!

EPILOGUE

"**G**o Baby! Go Baby!" Sugar chanted and cheered her son on as she watched him live on the news from her hotel room being chased down rt. 40 after busting shots at the squad cars to get them off his ass. They had the helicopter tailing him, so she knew that nine times out of ten, it was only a matter of time before the police trapped him off, because it was almost impossible to get away from a chopper. She just hoped that he would take out as many of those cock-sucking pigs as he could before he went out like she knew her warrior of a son would, in a blaze of glory!

When Tee made it in front of their apartment building and slid out of his car and onto the ground swinging his machine gun every which way before being riddled with bullets by what looked to be the entire New Castle County Police Force, Sugar shed a few tears, then quickly wiped her eyes. This wasn't a situation for her to mourn over. Sugar was a Gangstress, and although she didn't want that life for Tee, a young Gangsta was what he came out to be with a purpose to make sure his mother was good. So, Sugar couldn't cry tears of mourning and pain when her baby went out like a certified gangsta, because he fulfilled his purpose. Sugar was Tee's bank, and he had it that was so that if he ever had to turn in and do a bid or got gunned down in the streets, his mother would have his earnings to live off of. A quarter million dollars wasn't enough to last Sugar a lifetime, but she knew exactly what to do with it.

She looked up and said, "Thank you Baby!
Mommy love you...."

YOUNG   CANNON!!

SNEAK PREVIEW

OF YOUNG CANNON II: A Mother's Revenge.....

AVAILABLE NOW!!!

"Tee went out blazin', but the story aint over/ Since her son died, Sug heart done grew colder/ Now she on her shit, Sug bouta hit the streets again/ So, she hit the plug, told him that she gotta meet wit' 'em/ Then she wrote a letter out to Tee friend Wacko/ He booked for a body, but she said she got his back though/ This was Tee right hand man, they ran the hood together/ So, to make sure that he good she gon' do whatever..."

~ Sadaam Hasaan

CHAPTER 1

"My baby went out like a fuckin' G!" Sugar shouted as she stood up from the bed in her hotel room and wiped the tears that had just fell from her eyes.

Sug was a 37 year old, mocha complexioned gangstress, standing 5'3, 154 lbs. with a well-proportioned body that looked like it belonged on the cover of Smooth Girl Magazine. Although Sug had her own long, growing hair, she alternated wigs. There was no way you could even tell that she was kicking 40 in the ass, as Sug didn't look a day over 21. Shit, she still got carded at the liquor stores.

Unfortunately, she had just watched her 16 year old son, Tee, live on TV getting gunned down by the police right in front of their Lexington Green apartment building. It was a bittersweet feeling for Sugar! The bitter was obvious, but the sweet came from the fact that he took about 6 or 7 pigs with him. He didn't just lay down like most so called "Gangsters" do; he went out in a blaze of glory! In her eyes, Tee was victorious! He did some real live Gangsta shit! So, Sugar being the natural born gangstress that she was, had to be proud of her son's final stand-off. He also left Sugar with over 200 grand of his winnings. She believed that Tee was going to "Gangsta's Paradise!"

~ ~ ~

Sugar didn't return home to her apartment in "Lex" (Lexington Green). She already had everything of value with her, because she never intended on going back home in the first place. Tee had acquired a lot of enemies and unwanted attention on his rise to fame, and with what Sugar planned on doing, Lex wasn't the place where she wanted to be resting her head at night. She moved to a one bedroom apartment in Pine Valley

Apartments off the rt. 13/rt. 40 split the day after Tee's funeral.

Once Sugar got settled into her new apartment, she sat down to write Tee's right hand man, "Wacko", a letter. He was only 17 years old, but the courts had waived him up to an adult, and he was facing a life bid without the possibility of parole for an alleged murder he committed in front of some eyewitnesses on "Da' Ave." (New Castle Ave.).

Dear Wacko,

I don't know if you heard, but Tee was killed during a shootout with the pigs a couple weeks ago. He went how he was supposed to go though. You would've definitely been proud of him. He took 3 of those motherfucka's with him. So, I know I was proud of my baby!

Anyway, I wanted to reach out to you to let you know I put my attorney on ya' case, and I'm covering the fees. He should be coming to visit you any day now if he hasn't already.

I'm also enclosing a $500 money order to hold you over. If you need anything else just let me know.

You got my cell number so put it on ya' list. You can call whenever. And I'll come see you soon so we can talk in person. Stay true to who you are Babyboy. I'm in the car with you, and I'm back on my shit!

Loyalty is Everything!

COMING SOON

1. The ultimate Checkmate (By K TYLER)

2. Sins of a Father (By Gregory Royal)

3. The Cost: More Than Just A Number (By D'Preme)